Marx
Hardy
Defoe
Abbott
Melville
Montaigne
Machiavelli
Haggard
Chesterton
Cooper
Emerson
Joyce
Austen
Hugo
Eliot
Grimm
Molière
Stoker
Carroll
Christie
Wilde
Maupassant
Byron
Engels
Schiller
Smith
Garnett
Hawthorne
Kafka
Goethe
Einstein
Fitzgerald
Dostoyevsky
Hall
Cotton
Kipling
Doyle
Willis
Baum
Henry
Nietzsche
Leslie
Dumas
Flaubert
Turgenev
Balzac
Stockton
Vatsyayana
Crane
Burroughs
Verne
Curtis
Tocqueville
Vinci
Homer
Widger
Tolstoy
Gogol
Busch
Darwin
Whitman
Twain
Scott
Potter
Thoreau
Plato
Harte
Freud
Zola
Lawrence
Kant
Jowett
Stevenson
Dickens
Burton
Hesse
Andersen
London
Descartes
Cervantes
Voltaire
Burton
Poe
Aristotle
Wells
Cooke
Hale
James
Hastings
Bunner
Shakespeare
Irving
Richter
Chambers
da
Doré
Chekhov
Shaw
Benedict
Alcott
Swift
Dante
Wodehouse
Pushkin
Newton

 **tredition®**

tredition was established in 2006 by Sandra Latusseck and Soenke Schulz. Based in Hamburg, Germany, tredition offers publishing solutions to authors and publishing houses, combined with world-wide distribution of printed and digital book content. tredition is uniquely positioned to enable authors and publishing houses to create books on their own terms and without conventional manu-facturing risks.

For more information please visit: www.tredition.com

TREDITION CLASSICS

This book is part of the TREDITION CLASSICS series. The creators of this series are united by passion for literature and driven by the intention of making all public domain books available in printed format again - worldwide. Most TREDITION CLASSICS titles have been out of print and off the bookstore shelves for decades. At tredition we believe that a great book never goes out of style and that its value is eternal. Several mostly non-profit literature projects provide content to tredition. To support their good work, tredition donates a portion of the proceeds from each sold copy. As a reader of a TREDITION CLASSICS book, you support our mission to save many of the amazing works of world literature from oblivion. See all available books at www.tredition.com.

Project Gutenberg

The content for this book has been graciously provided by Project Gutenberg. Project Gutenberg is a non-profit organization founded by Michael Hart in 1971 at the University of Illinois. The mission of Project Gutenberg is simple: To encourage the creation and distribution of eBooks. Project Gutenberg is the first and largest collection of public domain eBooks.

What Will He Do with It?

Volume 8

Baron Edward Bulwer Lytton Lytton

Imprint

This book is part of TREDITION CLASSICS

Author: Baron Edward Bulwer Lytton Lytton
Cover design: Buchgut, Berlin – Germany

Publisher: tredition GmbH, Hamburg - Germany
ISBN: 978-3-8424-3107-2

www.tredition.com
www.tredition.de

Copyright:
The content of this book is sourced from the public domain.

The intention of the TREDITION CLASSICS series is to make world literature in the public domain available in printed format. Literary enthusiasts and organizations, such as Project Gutenberg, world-wide have scanned and digitally edited the original texts. tredition has subsequently formatted and redesigned the content into a modern reading layout. Therefore, we cannot guarantee the exact reproduction of the original format of a particular historic edition. Please also note that no modifications have been made to the spelling, therefore it may differ from the orthography used today.

BOOK VIII.

CHAPTER I.

"A LITTLE FIRE BURNS UP A GREAT DEAL OF CORN." — OLD PROVERB.

Guy Darrell resumed the thread of solitary life at Fawley with a calm which was deeper in its gloom than it had been before. The experiment of return to the social world had failed. The resolutions which had induced the experiment were finally renounced. Five years nearer to death, and the last hope that had flitted across the narrowing passage to the grave, fallen like a faithless torch from his own hand, and trodden out by his own foot.

It was peculiarly in the nature of Darrell to connect his objects with posterity — to regard eminence in the Present but as a beacon-height from which to pass on to the Future the name he had taken from the Past. All his early ambition, sacrificing pleasure to toil, had placed its goal at a distance, remote from the huzzas of bystanders; and Ambition halted now, baffled and despairing. Childless, his line would perish with himself — himself, who had so vaunted its restoration in the land! His genius was childless also — it would leave behind it no offspring of the brain. By toil he had amassed ample wealth; by talent he had achieved a splendid reputation. But the reputation was as perishable as the wealth. Let a half-century pass over his tomb, and nothing would be left to speak of the successful lawyer the applauded orator, save traditional anecdotes, a laudatory notice in contemporaneous memoirs — perhaps, at most, quotations of eloquent sentences lavished on forgotten cases and obsolete debates — shreds and fragments of a great intellect, which another half-century would sink without a bubble into the depths of Time. He had enacted no laws — he had administered no state — he had composed no books. Like the figure on a clock, which adorns

the case and has no connection with the movement, he, so promi-
nent an or nament to time, had no part in its works. Removed, the
eye would miss him for a while; but a nation's literature or history
was the same, whether with him or without. Some with a tithe of
his abilities have the luck to fasten their names to things that en-
dure; they have been responsible for measures they did not not
invent, and which, for good or evil, influence long generations.
They have written volumes out of which a couplet of verse, a period
in prose, may cling to the rock of ages, as a shell that survives a
deluge. But the orator, whose effects are immediate—who enthralls
his audience in proportion as he nicks the hour—who, were he
speaking like Burke what, apart from the subject-matter, closet stu-
dents would praise, must, like Burke, thin his audience, and exchange present oratorical success for ultimate intellectual renown—
a man, in short, whose oratory is emphatically that of the DEBATER
is, like an actor, rewarded with a loud applause and a complete
oblivion. Waife on the village stage might win applause no less
loud, followed by oblivion not more complete.

Darrell was not blind to the brevity of his fame. In his previous
seclusion he had been resigned to that conviction—now it saddened
him. Then, unconfessed by himself, the idea that he might yet reap-
pear in active life, and do something which the world would not
willingly let die, had softened the face of that tranquil Nature from
which he must soon now pass out of reach and sight. On the tree of
Time he was a leaf already sear upon the bough—not an inscription
graven into the rind.

Ever slow to yield to weak regrets—ever seeking to combat his
own enemies within—Darrell said to himself one night, while
Fairthorn's flute was breathing an air of romance through the melancholy walls: "Is it too late yet to employ this still busy brain upon
works that will live when I am dust, and make Posterity supply the
heir that fails to my house?"

He shut himself up with immortal authors—he meditated on the
choice of a theme; his knowledge was wide, his taste refined;—
words!—he could not want words! Why should he not write? Alas;
why indeed?—He who has never been a writer in his youth, can no
more be a writer in his age than he can be a painter—a musician.

What! not write a book! Oh, yes—as he may paint a picture or set a song. But a writer, in the emphatic sense of the word—a writer as Darrell was an orator—oh, no! And, least of all, will he be a writer if he has been an orator by impulse and habit— an orator too happily gifted to require, and too laboriously occupied to resort to, the tedious aids of written preparation—an orator as modern life forms orators—not, of course, an orator like those of the classic world, who elaborated sentences before delivery, and who, after delivery, polished each extemporaneous interlude into rhetorical exactitude and musical perfection. And how narrow the range of compositions to a man burdened already by a grave reputation! He cannot have the self- abandonment—he cannot venture the headlong charge— with which Youth flings the reins to genius, and dashes into the ranks of Fame. Few and austere his themes—fastidious and hesitating his taste. Restricted are the movements of him who walks for the first time into the Forum of Letters with the purple hem on his senatorial toga. Guy Darrell, at his age, entering among authors as a novice!—he, the great lawyer, to whom attorneys would have sent no briefs had he been suspected of coquetting with a muse,—he, the great orator who had electrified audiences in proportion to the sudden effects which distinguish oral inspiration from written eloquence—he achieve now, in an art which his whole life had neglected, any success commensurate to his contemporaneous repute;— how unlikely! But a success which should outlive that repute, win the "everlasting inheritance" which could alone have nerved him to adequate effort—how impossible! He could not himself comprehend why, never at a loss for language felicitously opposite or richly ornate when it had but to flow from his thought to his tongue, nor wanting ease, even eloquence, in epistolary correspondence confidentially familiar—he should find words fail ideas, and ideas fail words, the moment his pen became a wand that conjured up the Ghost of the dread Public! The more copious his thoughts, the more embarrassing their selection; the more exquisite his perception of excellence in others, the more timidly frigid his efforts at faultless style. It would be the same with the most skilful author, if the Ghost of the Public had not long since ceased to haunt him. While he writes, the true author's solitude is absolute or peopled at his will. But take an audience from an orator, what is he? He commands the living public—the Ghost of the Public awes himself.

"Surely once," sighed Darrell, as he gave his blurred pages to the flames—" surely once I had some pittance of the author's talent, and have spent it upon lawsuits!"

The author's talent, no doubt, Guy Darrell once had—the author's temperament never. What is the author's temperament? Too long a task to define. But without it a man may write a clever book, a useful book, a book that may live a year, ten years, fifty years. He will not stand out to distant ages a representative of the age that rather lived in him than he in it. The author's temperament is that which makes him an integral, earnest, original unity, distinct from all before and all that may succeed him. And as a Father of the Church has said that the consciousness of individual being is the sign of immortality, not granted to the inferior creatures—so it is in this individual temperament one and indivisible, and in the intense conviction of it, more than in all the works it may throw off, that the author becomes immortal. Nay, his works may perish like those of Orpheus or Pythagoras; but he himself, in his name, in the footprint of his being, remains, like Orpheus or Pythagoras, undestroyed, indestructible.

Resigning literature, the Solitary returned to Science. There he was more at home. He had cultivated science, in his dazzling academical career, with ardour and success; he had renewed the study, on his first retirement to Fawley, as a distraction from tormenting memories or unextin guished passions. He now for the first time regarded the absorbing abstruse occupation as a possible source of fame. To be one in the starry procession of those sons of light who have solved a new law in the statute-book of heaven! Surely a grand ambition, not unbecoming to his years and station, and pleasant in its labours to a man who loved Nature's outward scenery with poetic passion, and had studied her inward mysteries with a sage's minute research. Science needs not the author's art—she rejects its gracess—he recoils with a shudder from its fancies. But Science requires in the mind of the discoverer a limpid calm. The lightnings that reveal Diespiter must flash in serene skies. No clouds store that thunder

> "Quo bruta tellus, et vaga flumina,
> Quo Styx, et invisi horrida Taenari

Sedes, Atlanteusque finis
Concutitur!"

So long as you take science only as a distraction, science will not
lead you to discovery. And from some cause or other, Guy Darrell
was more unquiet and perturbed in his present than in his past
seclusion. Science this time failed even to distract. In the midst of
august meditations— of close experiment—some haunting angry
thought from the far world passed with rude shadow between Intellect and Truth—the heart eclipsed the mind. The fact is, that Darrell's genius was essentially formed for Action. His was the true
orator's temperament, with the qualities that belong to it—the grasp
of affairs—the comprehension of men and states —the constructive,
administrative faculties. In such career, and in such career alone,
could he have developed all his powers, and achieved an imperish-
able name. Gradually as science lost its interest, he retreated from
all his former occupations, and would wander for long hours over
the wild unpopulated landscapes round him. As if it were his object
to fatigue the body, and in that fatigue tire out the restless brain, he
would make his gun the excuse for rambles from sunrise to twilight
over the manors he had purchased years ago, lying many miles off
from Fawley. There are times when a man who has passed his life in
cultivating his mind finds that the more he can make the physical
existence predominate, the more he can lower himself to the rude
vigour of the gamekeeper, or his day-labourer—why, the more he
can harden his nerves to support the weight of his reflections.

In these rambles he was not always alone. Fairthorn contrived to
insinuate himself much more than formerly into his master's habitual companionship. The faithful fellow had missed Darrell so sorely
in that long unbroken absence of five years, that on recovering him,
Fairthorn seemed resolved to make up for lost time. Departing from
his own habits, he would, therefore, lie in wait for Guy Darrell—
creeping out of a bramble or bush, like a familiar sprite; and was no
longer to be awed away by a curt syllable or a contracted brow. And
Darrell, at first submitting reluctantly, and out of compassionate
kindness to the flute- player's obtrusive society, became by degrees
to welcome and relax in it. Fairthorn knew the great secrets of his
life. To Fairthorn alone on all earth could he speak with out reserve

of one name and of one sorrow. Speaking to Fairthorn was like talking to himself, or to his pointers, or to his favourite doe, upon which last he bestowed a new collar, with an inscription that implied more of the true cause that had driven him a second time to the shades of Fawley than he would have let out to Alban Morley or even to Lionel Haughton. Alban was too old for that confidence —Lionel much too young. But the Musician, like Art itself, was of no age; and if ever the gloomy master unbent his outward moodiness and secret spleen in any approach to gaiety, it was in a sort of saturnine playfulness to this grotesque, grown-up infant. They cheered each other, and they teased each other. Stalking side by side over the ridged fallows, Darrell would sometimes pour forth his whole soul, as a poet does to his muse; and at Fairthorn's abrupt interruption or rejoinder, turn round on him with fierce objurgation or withering sarcasm, or what the flute-player abhorred more than all else, a truculent quotation from Horace, which drove Fairthorn away into some vanishing covert or hollow, out of which Darrell had to entice him, sure that, in return, Fairthorn would take a sly occasion to send into his side a vindictive prickle. But as the two came home in the starlight, the dogs dead beat and poor Fairthorn too, —ten to one but what the musician was leaning all his weight on his master's nervous arm, and Darrell was looking with tender kindness in the face of the SOMEONE left to lean upon him still.

One evening, as they were sitting together in the library, the two hermits, each in his corner, and after a long silence, the flute-player said abruptly

"I have been thinking —"

"Thinking!" quoth Darrell, with his mechanical irony; "I am sorry for you. Try not to do so again."

FAIRTHORN. —"Your poor dear father —"

DARRELL (wincing, startled, and expectant of a prickle). —"Eh? my father —"

FAIRTHORN. —"Was a great antiquary. How it would have pleased him could he have left a fine collection of antiquities as an heirloom to the nation! —his name thus preserved for ages, and connected with the studies of his life. There are the Elgin Marbles.

The parson was talking to me yesterday of a new Vernon Gallery; why not in the British Museum an everlasting Darrell room? Plenty to stock it mouldering yonder in the chambers which you will never finish."

"My dear Dick," Said Darrell, starting up, "give me your hand. What a brilliant thought! I could do nothing else to preserve my dear father's name. Eureka! You are right. Set the carpenters at work to-morrow. Remove the boards; open the chambers; we will inspect their stores, and select what would worthily furnish 'A Darrell Room.' Perish Guy Darrell the lawyer! Philip Darrell the antiquary at least shall live!"

It is marvellous with what charm Fairthorn's lucky idea seized upon Darrell's mind. The whole of the next day he spent in the forlorn skeleton of the unfinished mansion slowly decaying beside his small and homely dwelling. The pictures, many of which were the rarest originals in early Flemish and Italian art, were dusted with tender care, and hung from hasty nails upon the bare ghastly walls. Delicate ivory carvings, wrought by the matchless hand of Cellini-early Florentine bronzes, priceless specimens of Raffaele ware and Venetian glass—the precious trifles, in short, which the collector of mediaeval curiosities amasses for his heirs to disperse amongst the palaces of kings and the cabinets of nations—were dragged again to unfamiliar light. The invaded sepulchral building seemed a very Pompeii of the /Cinque Cento/. To examine, arrange, methodise, select for national purposes, such miscellaneous treasures would be the work of weeks. For easier access, Darrell caused a slight hasty passage to be thrown over the gap between the two edifices. It ran from the room nicked into the gables of the old house, which, originally fitted up for scientific studies, now became his habitual apartment, into the largest of the uncompleted chambers which had been designed for the grand reception-gallery of the new building. Into the pompous gallery thus made contiguous to his monk-like cell, he gradually gathered the choicest specimens of his collection. The damps were expelled by fires on grateless hearthstones; sunshine admitted from windows now for the first time exchanging boards for glass; rough iron sconces, made at the nearest forge, were thrust into the walls, and sometimes lighted at night-Darrell and Fairthorn walking arm-in-arm along the unpolished floors, in company with Holbein's Nobles, Perugino's Virgins. Some of that high-bred company displaced and banished the next day, as repeated inspection made the taste more rigidly exclusive. Darrell had found object, amusement, occupation—frivolous if Compared with those lenses, and glasses, and algebraical scrawls which had once whiled lonely hours in the attic-room hard by; but not frivolous even to the judgment of the austerest sage, if that sage had not reasoned away his heart. For here it was not Darrell's taste that was delighted; it was Darrell's heart that, ever hungry, had found food. His heart was connecting those long-neglected memorials of an ambition baffled and relinquished—here with a nation, there with his father's grave! How his eyes sparkled! how his lip smiled! Nobody would have guessed it—none of us know each other; least of all do we know the interior being of those whom we estimate by public repute;—but what a world of simple, fond affection lay coiled and wasted in that proud man's solitary breast!

CHAPTER II.

THE LEARNED COMPUTE THAT SEVEN HUNDRED AND SEVEN MILLIONS OF MILLIONS OF VIBRATIONS HAVE PENETRATED THE EYE BEFORE THE EYE CAN DISTINGUISH THE TINTS OF A VIOLET. WHAT PHILOSOPHY CAN CAL-CULATE THE VIBRATIONS OF THE HEART BEFORE IT CAN DISTINGUISH THE COLOURS OF LOVE?

While Guy Darrell thus passed his hours within the unfinished fragments of a dwelling builded for posterity, and amongst the still relics of remote generations, Love and Youth were weaving their warm eternal idyll on the sunny lawns by the gliding river.

There they are, Love and Youth, Lionel and Sophy, in the arbour round which her slight hands have twined the honeysuckle, fond imitation of that bower endeared by the memory of her earliest holiday—she seated coyly, he on the ground at her feet, as when Titania had watched his sleep. He has been reading to her, the book has fallen from his hand. What book? That volume of poems so unintelligibly obscure to all but the dreaming young, who are so unintelligibly obscure to themselves. But to the merit of those po-ems, I doubt if even George did justice. It is not true, I believe, that they are not durable. Some day or other, when all the jargon so feelingly denounced by Colonel Morley about "esthetics," and "ob-jective," and "subjective," has gone to its long home, some critic who can write English will probably bring that poor little volume fairly before the public; and, with all its manifold faults, it will take a place in the affections, not of one single generation of the young, but —everlasting, ever-dreaming, ever-growing youth. But you and I, reader, have no other interest in these poems, except this—that they were written by the brother-in-law of that whimsical, miserly Frank Vance, who perhaps, but for such a brother-in-law, would never have gone through the labour by which he has cultivated the genius that achieved his fame; and if he had not cultivated that genius, he might never have known Lionel; and if he had never known Lionel, Lionel might never perhaps have gone to the Surrey village, in which he saw the Phenomenon: And, to push farther still that Voltaireian philosophy of ifs—if either Lionel or Frank Vance had not been so intimately associated in the minds of Sophy and Lionel with the golden holiday on the beautiful river, Sophy and Lionel might not have thought so much of those poems; and if they had not thought so much of those poems, there might not have been between them that link of poetry without which the love of two young people is a sentiment, always very pretty it is true, but much too commonplace to deserve special commemoration in a work so uncommonly long as this is likely to be. And thus it is clear that Frank Vance is not a superfluous and episodical personage amongst the characters of this history, but, however indirectly, still essentially, one of those beings without whom the author must have given a very different answer to the question, "What will he do with it?"

Return we to Lionel and Sophy. The poems have brought their hearts nearer and nearer together. And when the book fell from Lionel's hand, Sophy knew that his eyes were on her face, and her own eyes looked away. And the silence was so deep and so sweet! Neither had yet said to the other a word of love. And in that silence both felt that they loved and were beloved. Sophy! how childlike she looked still! How little she is changed!—except that the soft blue eyes are far more pensive, and that her merry laugh is now never heard. In that luxurious home, fostered with the tenderest care by its charming owner, the romance of her childhood realised, and Lionel by her side, she misses the old crippled vagrant. And therefore it is that her merry laugh is no longer heard! "Ah!" said Lionel, softly breaking the pause at length, "do not turn your eyes from me, or I shall think that there are tears in them!" Sophy's breast heaved, but her eyes were averted still. Lionel rose gently, and came to the other side of her quiet form. "Fie! there are tears, and you would hide them from me. Ungrateful!"

Sophy looked at him now with candid, inexpressible, guileless affection in those swimming eyes, and said with touching sweetness: "Ungrateful! Should I not be so if I were gay and happy?"

And in self-reproach for not being sufficiently unhappy while that young consoler was by her side, she too rose, left the arbour, and looked wistfully along the river. George Morley was expected;

he might bring tidings of the absent. And now while Lionel, rejoining her, exerts all his eloquence to allay her anxiety and encourage her hopes, and while they thus, in that divinest stage of love, ere the tongue repeats what the eyes have told, glide along-here in sunlight by lingering flowers- there in shadow under mournful willows, whose leaves are ever the latest to fall, let us explain by what links of circumstance Sophy became the great lady's guest, and Waife once more a homeless wanderer.

CHAPTER III.

COMPRISING MANY NEEDFUL EXPLANATIONS ILLUSTRATIVE OF WISE SAWS; AS FOR EXAMPLE, "HE THAT HATH AN ILL NAME IS HALF HANGED." "HE THAT HATH BEEN BITTEN BY A SERPENT IS AFRAID OF A ROPE." "HE THAT LOOKS FOR A STAR PUTS OUT HIS CANDLES;" AND, "WHEN GOD WILLS, ALL WINDS BRING RAIN."

The reader has been already made aware how, by an impulse of womanhood and humanity, Arabella Crane had been converted from a persecuting into a tutelary agent in the destinies of Waife and Sophy. That evolution in her moral being dated from the evening on which she had sought the cripple's retreat, to warn him of Jasper's designs. We have seen by what stratagem she had made it appear that Waife and his grandchild had sailed beyond the reach of molestation; with what liberality she had advanced the money that freed Sophy from the manager's claim; and how considerately she had empowered her agent to give the reference which secured to Waife the asylum in which we last beheld him. In a few stern sentences she had acquainted Waife with her fearless inflexible resolve to associate her fate henceforth with the life of his lawless son; and, by rendering abortive all his evil projects of plunder, to compel him at last to depend upon her for an existence neither unsafe nor sordid, provided only that it were not dishonest. The moment that she revealed that design, Waife's trust in her was won. His own heart enabled him to comprehend the effect produced upon a character otherwise unamiable and rugged, by the grandeur of self-immolation and the absorption of one devoted heroic thought. In the strength and bitterness of passion which thus pledged her existence to redeem another's, he obtained the key to her vehement and jealous nature; saw why she had been so cruel to the child of a rival; why she had conceived compassion for that child in proportion as the father's unnatural indifference had quenched the anger of her own self-love; and, above all, why, as the idea of reclaiming and appropriating solely to herself the man who, for good or for evil, had grown into the all-predominant object of her life, gained more and more the mastery over her mind, it expelled the lesser and the baser passions, and the old mean revenge against an infant faded away before the light of that awakening conscience which is often rekindled from ashes by the sparks of a single better and worthier thought. And in the resolute design to reclaim Jasper Losely, Arabella came at once to a ground in common with his father, with his child. Oh what, too, would the old man owe to her, what would be his gratitude, his joy, if she not only guarded his spotless Sophy, but saved from the bottomless abyss his guilty son! Thus when Arabella Crane had, nearly five years before, sought Waife's discovered hiding-place, near the old bloodstained Tower, mutual interests and sympathies had formed between them a bond of alliance not the less strong because rather tacitly acknowledged than openly expressed. Arabella had written to Waife from the Continent, for the first half-year pretty often, and somewhat sanguinely, as to the chance of Losely's ultimate reformation. Then the intervals of silence became gradually more prolonged, and the letters more brief. But still, whether from the wish not unnecessarily to pain the old man, or, as would be more natural to her character, which, even in its best aspects, was not gentle, from a proud dislike to confess failure, she said nothing of the evil courses which Jasper had renewed. Evidently she was always near him. Evidently, by some means or another, his life, furtive and dark, was ever under the glare of her watchful eyes.

Meanwhile Sophy had been presented to Caroline Montfort. As Waife had so fondly anticipated, the lone childless lady had taken with kindness and interest to the fair motherless child. Left to herself often for months together in the grand forlorn house, Caroline soon found an object to her pensive walks in the basket-maker's cottage. Sophy's charming face and charming ways stole more and more into affections which were denied all nourishment at home. She entered into Waife's desire to improve, by education, so exquisite a nature; and, familiarity growing by degrees, Sophy was at length coaxed up to the great house; and during the hours which Waife devoted to his rambles (for even in his settled industry he could not conquer his vagrant tastes, but would weave his reeds or osiers as he sauntered through solitudes of turf or wood), became the docile delighted pupil in the simple chintz room which Lady Montfort had reclaimed from the desert of her surrounding palace. Lady Montfort was not of a curious turn of mind; profoundly indifferent even to the gossip of drawing-rooms, she had no rankling desire to know the secrets of village hearthstones. Little acquainted even with the great world- scarcely at all with any world below that in which she had her being, save as she approached humble sorrows by delicate charity—the contrast between Waife's calling and his conversation roused in her no vigilant suspicions. A man of some education, and born in a rank that touched upon the order of gentlemen, but of no practical or professional culture —with whimsical tastes—with roving eccentric habits—had, in the course of life, picked up much harmless wisdom, but, perhaps from want of worldly prudence, failed of fortune. Contented with an obscure retreat and a humble livelihood, he might naturally be loth to confide to others the painful history of a descent in life. He might have relations in a higher sphere, whom the confession would shame; he might be silent in the manly pride which shrinks from alms and pity and a tale of fall. Nay, grant the worst—grant that Waife had suffered in repute as well as fortune—grant that his character had been tarnished by some plausible circumstantial evidences which he could not explain away to the satisfaction of friends or the acquittal of a short-sighted world—had there not been, were there not always, many innocent men similarly afflicted? And who could hear Waife talk, or look on his arch smile, and not feel that he was innocent? So, at least, thought Caroline Montfort. Naturally; for if, in her essentially woman-like character, there was one all-pervading and all-predominant attribute, it was PITY. Lead Fate placed her under circumstances fitted to ripen into genial development all her exquisite forces of soul, her true post in this life would have been that of the SOOTHER. What a child to some grief-worn father! What a wife to some toiling, aspiring, sensitive man of genius! What a mother to some suffering child! It seemed as if it were necessary to her to have something to compassionate and foster. She was sad when there was no one to comfort; but her smile was like a sunbeam from Eden when it chanced on a sorrow it could brighten away. Out of this very sympathy came her faults—faults of reasoning and judgment. Prudent in her own chilling path through what the world calls temptations, because so ineffably pure—because, to Fashion's light tempters, her very thought was as closed, as

"Under the glassy, cool, translucent wave,"

was the ear of Sabrina to the comrades of Comus,—yet place before her some gentle scheme that seemed fraught with a blessing for others, and straightway her fancy embraced it, prudence faded—she saw not the obstacles, weighed not the chances against it. Charity to her did not come alone, but with its sister twins, Hope and Faith.

Thus, benignly for the old man and the fair child, years rolled on till Lord Montfort's sudden death, and his widow was called upon to exchange Montfort Court (which passed to the new heir) for the distant jointure House of Twickenham. By this time she had grown so attached to Sophy, and Sophy so gratefully fond of her, that she proposed to Waife to take his sweet grandchild as her permanent companion, complete her education, and assure her future. This had been the old man's cherished day-dream; but he had not contemplated its realisation until he himself were in the grave. He turned pale, he staggered, when the proposal which would separate him from his grandchild was first brought before him. But he recovered ere Lady Montfort could be aware of the acuteness of the pang she inflicted, and accepted the generous offer with warm protestations of joy and gratitude. But Sophy! Sophy consent to leave her grandfather afar and aged in his solitary cottage! Little did either of them know Sophy, with her soft heart and determined soul, if they supposed such egotism possible in her. Waife insisted—Waife was angry—Waife was authoritative—Waife was imploring—Waife was pathetic—all in vain! But to close every argument, the girl went boldly to Lady Montfort, and said: "If I left him, his heart would break—never ask it." Lady Montfort kissed Sophy tenderly as mother ever kissed a child for some sweet loving trait of a noble nature, and said simply "But he shall not be left—he shall come too."

She offered Waife rooms in her Twickenham house—she wished to collect books—he should be librarian. The old man shivered and refused—refused firmly. He had made a vow not to be a guest in any house. Finally, the matter was compromised; Waife would remove to the neighbourhood of Twickenham; there hire a cottage;

there ply his art; and Sophy, living with him, should spend part of each day with Lady Montfort as now.

So it was resolved. Waife consented to occupy a small house on the verge of the grounds belonging to the jointure villa, on the condition of paying rent for it. And George Morley insisted on the privilege of preparing that house for his old teacher's reception, leaving it simple and rustic to outward appearance, but fitting its pleasant chambers with all that his knowledge of the old man's tastes and habits suggested for comfort or humble luxury; a room for Sophy, hung with the prettiest paper, all butterflies and flowers, commanding a view of the river. Waife, despite his proud scruples, could not refuse such gifts from a man whose fortune and career had been secured by his artful lessons. Indeed, he had already permitted George to assist, though not largely, his own efforts to repay the L100 advanced by Mrs. Crane. The years he had devoted to a craft which his ingenuity made lucrative, had just enabled the basketmaker, with his pupil's aid, to clear off that debt by instalments. He had the satisfaction of thinking that it was his industry that had replaced the sum to which his grandchild owed her release from the execrable Rugge.

Lady Montfort's departure (which preceded Waife's by some weeks) was more mourned by the poor in her immediate neighbourhood than by the wealthier families who composed what a province calls its society; and the gloom which that event cast over the little village round the kingly mansion was increased when Waife and his grandchild left.

For the last three years, emboldened by Lady Montfort's protection, and the conviction that he was no longer pursued or spied, the old man relaxed his earlier reserved and secluded habits. Constitutionally sociable, he had made acquaintance with his humbler neighbours; lounged by their cottage palings in his rambles down the lanes; diverted their children with Sir Isaac's tricks, or regaled them with nuts and apples from his little orchard; giving to the more diligent labourers many a valuable hint how to eke out the daily wage with garden produce, or bees, or poultry; doctored farmer's cows; and even won the heart of the stud- groom by a mysterious sedative ball, which had reduced to serene docility a highly nervous and hitherto unmanageable four-year-old. Sophy had been no less popular. No one grudged her the favour of Lady Montfort—no one wondered at it. They were loved and honoured. Perhaps the happiest years Waife had known since his young wife left the earth were passed in the hamlet which he fancied her shade haunted; for was it not there— there, in that cottage—there, in sight of those green osiers, that her first modest virgin replies to his letters of love and hope that soothed his confinement and animated him—till then little fond of sedentary toils—to the very industry which, learned in sport, now gave subsistence, and secured a home. To that home persecution had not come—gossip had not pryed into its calm seclusion—even chance, when threatening disclosure, had seemed to pass by innocuous. For once —a year or so before he left—an incident had occurred which alarmed him at the time, but led to no annoying results. The banks of the great sheet of water in Montfort Park were occasionally made the scene of rural picnics by the families of neighbouring farmers or tradesmen. One day Waife, while carelessly fashioning his baskets on his favourite spot, was recognised, on the opposite margin, by a party of such holiday-makers to whom he himself had paid no attention. He was told the next day by the landlady of the village inn, the main chimney of which he had undertaken to cure of smoking, that a "lady" in the picnic symposium of the day before had asked many questions about him and his grandchild, and had seemed pleased to hear they were both so comfortably settled. The "lady" had been accompanied by another "lady," and by two or three young gentlemen. They had arrived in a "buss," which they had hired for the occasion. They had come from Humberston the day after those famous races which annually filled Humberston with strangers—the time of year in which Rugge's grand theatrical exhibition delighted that ancient town. From the description of the two ladies Waife suspected that they belonged to Rugge's company.

But they had not claimed Waife as a ci-devant comrade; they had not spoken of Sophy as the Phenomenon or the Fugitive. No molestation followed this event; and, after all, the Remorseless Baron had no longer any claim to the Persecuted Bandit or to Juliet Araminta.

But the ex-comedian is gone from the osiers—the hamlet. He is in his new retreat by the lordly river—within an hour of the smoke and roar of tumultuous London. He tries to look cheerful and happy, but his repose is troubled—his heart is anxious. Ever since Sophy, on his account, refused the offer which would have transferred her, not for a few daily hours, but for habitual life, from a basket-maker's roof to all the elegancies and refinements of a sphere in which, if freed from him, her charms and virtues might win her some such alliance as seemed impossible, while he was thus dragging her down to his own level,—ever since that day the old man had said to himself, "I live too long." While Sophy was by his side he appeared busy at his work and merry in his humour; the moment she left him for Lady Montfort's house, the work dropped from his hands, and he sank into moody thought.

Waife had written to Mrs. Crane (her address then was at Paris) on removing to Twickenhain, and begged her to warn him should Jasper meditate a return to England, by a letter directed to him at the General Post-office, London. Despite his later trust in Mrs. Crane, he did not deem it safe to confide to her Lady Montfort's offer to Sophy, or the affectionate nature of that lady's intimacy with the girl now grown into womanhood. With that insight into the human heart, which was in him not so habitually clear and steadfast as to be always useful, but at times singularly if erratically lucid, he could not feel assured that Arabella Crane's ancient hate to Sophy (which, lessening in proportion to the girl's destitution, had only ceased when the stern woman felt, with a sentiment bordering on revenge, that it was to her that Sophy owed an asylum obscure and humble) might not revive, if she learned that the child of a detested rival was raised above the necessity of her protection, and brought within view of that station so much Loftier than her own, from which she had once rejoiced to know that the offspring of a marriage which had darkened her life was excluded. For indeed it had been only on Waife's promise that he would not repeat the attempt that had proved so abortive, to enforce Sophy's claim on Guy Darrell, that Arabella Crane had in the first instance resigned the child to his care. His care—his—an attainted outcast! As long as Arabella Crane could see in Sophy but an object of compassion, she might haughtily protect her; but, could Sophy become an object of envy, would that protection last? No, he did not venture to confide in Mrs. Crane further than to say that he and Sophy had removed from

Montfort village to the vicinity of London. Time enough to say more when Mrs. Crane returned to England; and then, not by letter, but in personal interview.

Once a month the old man went to London to inquire at the General Post- office for any communications his correspondent might there address to him. Only once, however, had he heard from Mrs. Crane since the announcement of his migration, and her note of reply was extremely brief, until in the fatal month of June, when Guy Darrell and Jasper Losely had alike returned, and on the same day, to the metropolis; and then the old man received from her a letter which occasioned him profound alarm. It apprised him not only that his terrible son was in England—in London; but that Jasper had discovered that the persons embarked for America were not the veritable Waife and Sophy whose names they had assumed. Mrs. Crane ended with these ominous words: "It is right to say now that he has descended deeper and deeper. Could you see him, you would wonder that I neither abandon him nor my resolve. He hates me worse than the gibbet. To me and not to the gibbet he shall pass—fitting punishment to both. I am in London, not in my old house, but near him. His confidant is my hireling. His life and his projects are clear to my eyes—clear as if he dwelt in glass. Sophy is now of an age in which, were she placed in the care of some person whose respectability could not be impunged, she could not be legally forced away against her will; but if under your roof, those whom Jasper has induced to institute a search, that he has no means to institute very actively himself, might make statements which (as you are already aware) might persuade others, though well-meaning, to assist him in separating her from you. He might publicly face even a police- court, if he thus hoped to shame the rich man into buying off an intolerable scandal. He might, in the first instance, and more probably, decoy her into his power through stealth; and what might become of her before she was recovered? Separate yourself from her for a time. It is you, notwithstanding your arts of disguise, that can be the more easily tracked. She, now almost a woman, will have grown out of recognition. Place her in some secure asylum until, at least, you hear from me again."

Waife read and re-read this epistle (to which there was no direction that enabled him to reply) in the private room of a little coffeehouse to which he had retired from the gaze and pressure of the street. The determination he had long brooded over now began to take shape—to be hurried on to prompt decision. On recovering his first shock, he formed and matured his plans. That same evening he saw Lady Montfort. He felt that the time had come when, for Sophy's sake, he must lift the veil from the obloquy on his own name. To guard against the same concession to Jasper's authority that had betrayed her at Gatesboro', it was necessary that he should explain the mystery of Sophy's parentage and position to Lady Montfort, and go through the anguish of denouncing his own son as the last person to whose hands she should be consigned. He approached this subject not only with a sense of profound humiliation, but with no unreasonable fear lest Lady Montfort might at once decline a charge which would possibly subject her retirement to a harassing invasion. But, to his surprise as well as relief, no sooner had he named Sophy's parentage than Lady Montfort evinced emotions of a joy which cast into the shade all more painful or discreditable associations. "Henceforth, believe me," she said, "your Sophy shall be my own child, my own treasured darling!—no humble companion—my equal as well as my charge. Fear not that any one shall tear her from me. You are right in thinking that my roof should be her home—that she should have the rearing and the station which she is entitled as well as fitted to adorn. But you must not part from her. I have listened to your tale; my experience of you supplies the defence you suppress—it reverses the judgment which has aspersed you. And more ardently than before, I press on you a refuge in the Home that will shelter your grandchild." Noble-hearted woman! and nobler for her ignorance of the practical world, in the proposal which would have blistered with scorching blushes the cheek of that Personification of all "Solemn Plausibilities," the House of Vipont! Gentleman Waife was not scamp enough to profit by the ignorance which sprang from generous virtue. But, repressing all argument, and appearing to acquiesce in the possibility of such an arrangement, he left her benevolent delight unsaddened—and before the morning he was gone. Gone in stealth, and by the starlight, as he had gone years ago from the bailiff's cottage-gone, for Sophy, in waking, to find, as she had found before, farewell lines, that commended hope and forbade grief. "It was," he wrote, "for both their sakes that he had set out on a tour of pleasant adventure. He nee-

ded it; he had felt his spirits droop of late in so humdrum and settled a life. And there was danger abroad — danger that his brief absence would remove. He had confided all his secrets to Lady Montfort; she must look on that kind lady as her sole guardian till he
return — as return he surely would; and then they would live happy
ever afterwards as in fairy tales. He should never forgive her if she
were silly enough to fret for him. He should not be alone; Sir Isaac
would take care of him. He was not without plenty of money-
savings of several months; if he wanted more, he would apply to
George Morley. He would write to her occasionally; but she must
not expect frequent letters; he might be away for months — what did
that signify? He was old enough to take care of himself; she was no
longer a child to cry her eyes out if she lost a senseless toy, or a stu-
pid old cripple. She was a young lady, and he expected to find her a
famous scholar when he returned." And so, with all flourish and
bravado, and suppressing every attempt at pathos, the old man
went his way, and Sophy, hurrying to Lady Montfort's, weeping,
distracted, imploring her to send in all directions to discover and
bring back the fugitive, was there detained a captive guest. But
Waife left a letter also for Lady Montfort, cautioning and adjuring
her, as she valued Sophy's safety from the scandal of Jasper's claim,
not to make any imprudent attempts to discover him. Such attempt
would only create the very publicity from the chance of which he
was seeking to escape. The necessity of this caution was so obvious
that Lady Montfort could only send her most confidential servant to
inquire guardedly in the neighbourhood, until she had summoned
George Morley from Humberston, and taken him into counsel. Waife had permitted her to relate to him, on strict promise of secrecy,
the tale he had confided to her. George entered with the deepest
sympathy into Sophy's distress; but he made her comprehend the
indiscretion and peril of any noisy researches. He promised that he
himself would spare no pains to ascertain the old man's hiding-
place, and see, at least, if he could not be persuaded either to return
or suffer her to join him, that he was not left destitute and comfortless. Nor was this an idle promise. George, though his inquiries
were unceasing, crippled by the restraint imposed on them, was so
acute in divining, and so active in following up each clue to the
wanderer's artful doublings, that more than once he had actually
come upon the track, and found the very spot where Waife or Sir

Isaac had been seen a few days before. Still, up to the day on which Morley had last reported progress, the ingenious ex-actor, fertile in all resources of stratagem and disguise, had baffled his research. At first, however, Waife had greatly relieved the minds of these anxious friends, and cheered even Sophy's heavy heart, by letters, gay though brief. These letters having, by their postmarks, led to his trace, he had stated, in apparent anger, that reason for discontinuing them. And for the last six weeks no line from him had been received. In fact, the old man, on resolving to consummate his self-abnegation, strove more and more to wean his grandchild's thoughts from his image. He deemed it so essential to her whole future that, now she had found a home in so secure and so elevated a sphere, she should gradually accustom herself to a new rank of life, from which he was an everlasting exile; should lose all trace of his very being; efface a connection that, ceasing to protect, could henceforth only harm and dishonour her, — that he tried, as it were, to blot himself out of the world which now smiled on her. He did not underrate her grief in its first freshness; he knew that, could she learn where he was, all else would be forgotten—she would insist on flying to him. But he continually murmured to himself: "Youth is ever proverbially short of memory; its sorrows poignant, but not enduring; now the wounds are already scarring over—they will not reopen if they are left to heal."

He had, at first, thought of hiding somewhere not so far but that once a-week, or once a-month, he might have stolen into the grounds, looked at the house that held her—left, perhaps, in her walks some little token of himself. But, on reflection, he felt that that luxury would be too imprudent, and it ceased to tempt him in proportion as he reasoned himself into the stern wisdom of avoiding all that could revive her grief for him. At the commencement of this tale, in the outline given of that grand melodrama in which Juliet Araminta played the part of the Bandit's Child, her efforts to decoy pursuit from the lair of the persecuted Mime were likened to the arts of the skylark to lure eye and hand from the nest of his young. More appropriate that illustration now to the parent- bird than then to the fledgling. Farther and farther from the nest in which all his love was centred fled the old man. What if Jasper did discover him now; that very discovery would mislead the pursuit from Sophy.

Most improbable that Losely would ever guess that they could become separated; still more improbable, unless Waife, imprudently lurking near her home, guided conjecture, that Losely should dream of seeking under the roof of the lofty peeress the child that had fled from Mr. Rugge.

Poor old man! his heart was breaking; but his soul was so brightly comforted that there, where many, many long miles off, I see him standing, desolate and patient, in the corner of yon crowded mar- ket- place, holding Sir Isaac by slackened string with listless hand — Sir Isaac unshorn, travel-stained, draggled, with drooping head and melancholy eyes — yea, as I see him there, jostled by the crowd, to whom, now and then, pointing to that huge pannier on his arm, filled with some homely pedlar wares, he mechanically mutters, "Buy" — yea, I say, verily, as I see him thus, I cannot draw near in pity — I see what the crowd does not — the shadow of an angel's wing over his grey head; and I stand reverentially aloof, with bated breath and bended knee.

CHAPTER IV.

A WOMAN TOO OFTEN REASONS FROM HER HEART—HENCE TWO-THIRDS OF HER MISTAKES AND HER TROUBLES. A MAN OF GENIUS, TOO, OFTEN REASONS FROM HIS HEART-WENCE, ALSO, TWO-THIRDS OF HIS TROUBLES AND MISTAKES. WHEREFORE, BETWEEN WOMAN AND GENIUS THERE IS A SYMPATHETIC AFFINITY; EACH HAS SOME INTUITIVE COMPREHENSION OF THE SECRETS OF THE OTHER, AND THE MORE FEMININE THE WOMAN, THE MORE EXQUISITE THE GENIUS, THE MORE SUBTLE THE INTELLIGENCE BETWEEN THE TWO. BUT NOTE WELL THAT THIS TACIT UNDERSTANDING BECOMES OBSCURED, IF HUMAN LOVE PASS ACROSS ITS RELATIONS. SHAKESPEARE INTERPRETS ARIGHT THE MOST INTRICATE RIDDLES IN WOMAN. A WOMAN WAS THE FIRST TO INTERPRET ARIGHT THE ART THAT IS LATENT IN SHAKESPEARE. BUT DID ANNE HATHAWAY AND SHAKESPEARE UNDERSTAND EACH OTHER?

Unobserved by the two young people, Lady Montfort sate watching them as they moved along the river banks. She was seated where Lionel had first seen her—in the kind of grassy chamber that had been won from the foliage and the sward, closed round with interlaced autumnal branches, save where it opened towards the water. If ever woman's brain can conceive and plot a scheme thoroughly pure from one ungentle, selfish thread in its web, in such a scheme had Caroline Montfort brought together those two fair young natures. And yet they were not uppermost in her thoughts as she now gazed on them; nor was it wholly for them that her eyes were filled with tears at once sweet, yet profoundly mournful— holy, and yet intensely human.

Women love to think themselves uncomprehended—nor often without reason in that foible; for man, howsoever sagacious, rarely does entirely comprehend woman, howsoever simple. And in this her sex has the advantage over ours. Our hearts are bare to their eyes, even though they can never know what have been our lives. But we may see every action of their lives, guarded and circumscribed in conventional forms, while their hearts will have many mysteries to which we can never have the key. But, in more than the ordinary sense of the word, Caroline Montfort never had been a woman uncomprehended. Nor even in her own sex did she possess one confidante. Only the outward leaves of that beautiful flower opened to the sunlight. The leaves round the core were gathered fold upon fold closely as when life itself was in the bud.

As all the years of her wedded existence her heart had been denied the natural household vents, so by some strange and unaccountable chance her intellect also seemed restrained and pent from its proper freedom and play. During those barren years, she had read—she had pondered—she had enjoyed a commune with those whose minds instruct others, and still her own intelligence, which in early youth had been characterised by singular vivacity and brightness, and which Time had enriched with every womanly accomplishment, seemed chilled and objectless. It is not enough that a mind should be cultured—it should have movement as well as culture. Caroline Montfort's lay quiescent like a beautiful form spellbound to repose, but not to sleep. Looking on her once, as he stood amongst a crowd whom her beauty dazzled, a poet said abruptly: "Were my guess not a sacrilege to one so spotless and so haughty, I should say that I had hit on the solution of an enigma that long perplexed me; and in the core of that queen of the lilies, could we strip the leaves folded round it, we should find Remorse."

Lady Montfort started; the shadow of another form than her own fell upon the sward. George Morley stood behind her, his finger on his lips." Hush," he said in a whisper, see, Sophy is looking for me up the river. I knew she would be—I stole this way on purpose—for I would speak to you before I face her questions."

"What is the matter? you alarm me," said Lady Montfort, on gaining a part of the grounds more remote from the river, to which George had silently led the way.

"Nay, my dear cousin, there is less cause for alarm than for anxious deliberation, and that upon more matters than those which directly relate to our poor fugitive. You know that I long shrunk from enlisting the police in aid of our search. I was too sensible of the pain and offence which such an application would occasion Waife — (let us continue so to call him) — and the discovery of it might even induce him to put himself beyond our reach, and quit England. But his prolonged silence, and my fears lest some illness or mishap might have befallen him, together with my serious apprehensions of the effect which unrelieved anxiety might produce on Sophy's health, made me resolve to waive former scruples. Since I last saw you I have applied to one of the higher police-officers accustomed to confidential investigations of a similar nature. The next day he came to tell me that he had learned that a friend of his, who had been formerly a distinguished agent in the detective police, had been engaged for months in tracking a person whom he conjectured to be the same as the one whom I had commissioned him to discover, and with somewhat less caution and delicacy than I had enjoined. The fugitive's real name had been given to this ex-agent — the cause for search, that he had abducted and was concealing his granddaughter from her father. It was easy for me to perceive why this novel search had hitherto failed, no suspicion being entertained that Waife had separated himself from Sophy, and the inquiry being therefore rather directed towards the grandchild than the grandfather. But that inquiry had altogether ceased of late, and for this terrible reason — a different section of the police had fixed its eye upon the father on whose behalf the search had been instituted. This Jasper Losely (ah! our poor friend might well shudder to think Sophy should fall into his hands!) haunts the resorts of the most lawless and formidable desperadoes of London. He appears to be a kind of authority amongst them; but there is no evidence that as yet he has committed himself to any participation in their habitual courses. He lives profusely, for a person in such society (regaling Daredevils whom he awes by a strength and courage which are described as extraordinary), but with out any visible means. It seems that the ex-agent, who had been thus previously employed in Jasper Losely's name, had been engaged, not by Jasper himself, but by a person in very respectable circumstances, whose name I have ascertained to be Poole. And the ex-agent deemed it right to acquaint this Mr. Poole with Jasper's evil character and ambiguous mode of life, and to intimate to his employer that it might not be prudent to hold any connection with such a man, and still less proper to assist in restoring a young girl to his care. On this Mr. Poole became so much agitated, and expressed himself so incoherently as to his relations with Jasper, that the ex-agent conceived suspicions against Poole himself, and reported the whole circumstances to one of the chiefs of the former service, through whom they reached the very man whom I myself was employing. But this ex-agent, who had, after his last interview with Poole, declined all further interference, had since then, through a correspondent in a country town, whom he had employed at the first, obtained a clue to my dear old friend's wanderings, more recent, and I think more hopeful, than any I had yet discovered. You will remember that when questioning Sophy as to any friends in her former life to whom it was probable Waife might have addressed himself, she could think of no one so probable as a cobbler named Merle, with whom he and she had once lodged, and of whom he had often spoken to her with much gratitude as having put him in the way of recovering herself, and having shown him a peculiar trustful kindness on tha+ occasion. But you will remember also that I could not find this Merle; he had left the village, near this very place, in which he had spent the greater part of his lifehis humble trade having been neglected in consequence of some strange superstitious occupations in which, as he had gown older, he had become more and more absorbed. He had fallen into poverty, his effects had been sold off; he had gone away no one knew whither. Well, the ex-agent, who had also been directed to this Merle by his employer, had, through his correspondent, ascertained that the cobbler was living at Norwich, where he passed under the name of the Wise Man, and where he was in perpetual danger of being sent to the house of correction as an impostor, dealing in astrology, crystal-seeing, and such silly or nefarious practices. Very odd, indeed, and very melancholy, too," quoth the scholar, lifting up his hands and eyes, "that a man so gifted as our poor friend should ever have cultivated an acquaintance with a cobbler who deals in the Black Art!"

"Sophy has talked to me much about that cobbler," said Lady Montfort, with her sweet half-smile. "It was under his roof that she first saw Lionel Haughton. But though the poor man may be an ignorant enthusiast, he is certainly, by her account, too kind and simple-hearted to be a designing impostor."

GEORGE. — "Possibly. But to go on with my story: A few weeks ago, an elderly lame man, accompanied by a dog, who was evidently poor dear Sir Isaac, lodged two days with Merle at Norwich. On hearing this, I myself went yesterday to Norwich, saw and talked to Merle, and through this man I hope, more easily, delicately, and expeditiously than by any other means, to achieve our object. He evidently can assist us, and, as evidently, Waife has not told him that he is flying from Sophy and friends, but from enemies and persecutors. For Merle, who is impervious to bribes, and who at first was churlish and rude, became softened as my honest affection for the fugitive grew clear to him, and still more when I told him how wretched Sophy was at her grandfather's disappearance, and that she might fret herself into a decline. And we parted with this promise on his side, that if I would bring "down to him either Sophy herself (which is out of the question) or a line from her, which, in referring to any circumstances while under his roof that could only be known to her and himself, should convince him that the letter was from her hand, assuring him that it was for Waife's benefit and at her prayer that he should bestir himself in search for her grandfather, and that he might implicitly trust to me, he would do all he could to help us. So far, then, so good. But I have now more to say, and that is in reference to Sophy herself. While we are tracking her grandfather, the peril to her is not lessened. Never was that peril thoroughly brought before my eyes until I had heard actually from the police agent the dreadful character and associations of the man who can claim her in a fathers name. Waife, it is true, had told you that his son was profligate, spendthrift, lawless — sought her, not from natural affection, but as an instrument to be used, roughly and coarsely, for the purpose of extorting money from Mr. Darrell. But this stops far short of the terrible reality. Imagine the effect on her nerves, so depressed as they now are, nay, on her very life, should this audacious miscreant force himself here and say, 'Come with me, you are my child.' And are we quite sure that out of some refining ncbleness of conscience she might not imagine it her duty to obey, and to follow him? The more abject and friendless his condition, the more she might deem it her duty to be by his side. I have studied her from her childhood. She is capable of any error in judgment, if it be made to appear a martyr's devoted self-sacrifice. You may well shudder, my dear cousin. But grant that she were swayed by us and by the argument that so to act would betray and kill her beloved grandfather, still, in resisting this ruffian's paternal authority, what violent and painful scenes might ensue! What dreadful publicity to be attached for ever to her name! Nor is this all. Grant that her father does not discover her, but that he is led by his associates into some criminal offence, and suffers by the law — her relationship, both to him from whom you would guard her, and to him whose hearth you have so tenderly reared her to grace, suddenly dragged to day — would not the shame kill her? And in that disclosure how keen would be the anguish of Darrell!"

"Oh, heavens!" cried Caroline Montfort, white as ashes and wringing her hands, "you freeze me with terror. But this man cannot be so fallen as you describe. I have seen him — spoken with him in his youth — hoped then to assist in a task of conciliation, pardon. Nothing about him then foreboded so fearful a corruption. He might be vain, extravagant, selfish, false — Ah, yes! he was false indeed! but still the ruffian you paint, banded with common criminals, cannot be the same as the gay, dainty, perfumed, fair-faced adventurer with whom my ill-fated playmate fled her father's house. You shake your head — what is it you advise?"

"To expedite your own project — to make at once the resolute attempt to secure to this poor child her best, her most rightful protector — to let whatever can be done to guard her from danger or reclaim her father from courses to which despair may be driving him — to let, I say, all this be done by the person whose interest in doing it effectively is so paramount — whose ability to judge of and decide on the wisest means is so immeasurably superior to all that lies within our own limited experience of life."

"But you forget that our friend told me that he had appealed to — to Mr. Darrell on his return 'to England: that Mr. Darrell had peremptorily refused to credit the claim; and had sternly said that, even if Sophy's birth could be proved, he would not place under his father's roof the grandchild of William Losely."

"True; and yet you hoped reasonably enough to succeed where he, poor outcast, had failed."

"Yes, yes; I did hope that Sophy—her manners formed, her education completed—all her natural exquisite graces so cultured and refined, as to justify pride in the proudest kindred—I did so hope that she should be brought, as it were by accident, under his notice; that she would interest and charm him; and that the claim, when made, might thus be welcomed with delight. Mr. Darrell's abrupt return to a seclusion so rigid forbids the opportunity that ought easily have been found or made if he had remained in London. But suddenly, violently to renew a claim that such a man has rejected, before he has ever seen that dear child- before his heart and his taste plead for her—who would dare to do it? or, if so daring, who could hope success?"

"My dear Lady Montfort, my noble cousin, with repute as spotless as the ermine of your robe—who but you?"

"Who but I? Any one. Mr. Darrell would not even read through a letter addressed to him by me."

George stared with astonishment. Caroline's face was downcast—her attitude that of profound humiliated dejection.

"Incredible!" said he at length. "I have always suspected, and so indeed has my uncle, that Darrell had some cause of complaint against your mother. Perhaps he might have supposed that she had not sufficiently watched over his daughter, or had not sufficiently inquired into the character of the governess whom she recommended to him; and that this had led to an estrangement between Darrell and your mother, which could not fail to extend somewhat to yourself. But such misunderstandings can surely now be easily removed. Talk of his not reading a letter addressed to him by you! Why, do I not remember, when I was on a visit to my schoolfellow, his son, what influence you, a mere child yourself, had over that grave, busy man, then in the height of his career—how you alone could run without awe into his study—how you alone had the privilege to arrange his books, sort his papers—so that we two boys looked on you with a solemn respect, as the depositary of all his state secrets—how vainly you tried to decoy that poor timid Matilda, his daughter, into a share of your own audacity!—Is not all this true?"

"Oh yes, yes—old days gone for ever!"

"Do I not remember how you promised that, before I went back to school, I should hear Darrell read aloud—how you brought the volume of Milton to him in the evening—how he said, 'No, to-morrow night; I must now go to the House of Commons'—how I marvelled to hear you answer boldly, 'To-morrow night George will have left us, and I have promised that he shall hear you read'—and how, looking at you under those dark brows with serious softness, he said: 'Right: promises once given, must be kept. But was it not rash to promise in another's name?'—and you answered, half gently, half pettishly, 'As if you could fail me!' He took the book without another word, and read. What reading it was too! And do you not remember another time, how—"

LADY MONTFORT (interrupting with nervous impatience).—"Ay, ay—I need no reminding of all—all! Kindest, noblest, gentlest friend to a giddy, heedless child, unable to appreciate the blessing. But now, George, I dare not, I cannot write to Mr. Darrell."

George mused a moment, and conjectured that Lady Montfort had, in the inconsiderate impulsive season of youth, aided in the clandestine marriage of Darrell's daughter, and had become thus associated in his mind with the affliction that had embittered his existence. Were this so, certainly she would not be the fitting, inter-cessor on behalf of Sophy. His thoughts then turned to his uncle, Darrell's earliest friend, not suspecting that Colonel Morley was actually the person whom Darrell had already appointed his advi-ser and representative in all transactions that might concern the very parties under discussion. But just as he was about to suggest the expediency of writing to Alban to return to England, and taking him into confidence and consultation, Lady Montfort resumed, in a calmer voice and with a less troubled countenance:

"Who should be the pleader for one whose claim, if acknow-ledged, would affect his own fortunes, but Lionel Haughton?—Hold!—look where yonder they come into sight—there by the gap in the evergreens. May we not hope that Providence, bringing those two beautiful lives together, gives a solution to the difficulties which thwart our action and embarrass our judgment? I conceived and planned a blissful romance the first moment I gathered fran Sophy's artless confidences the effect that had been produced on her whole train of thought and feeling by the first meeting with Lionel in her childhood; by his brotherly, chivalrous kindness, and, above all, by the chance words he let fall, which discontented her with a life of shift and disguise, and revealed to her the instincts of her own holiest truthful nature. An alliance between Lionel Haughton and Sophy seemed to me the happiest possible event that could befall Guy Darrell. The two branches of his family united — a painful household secret confined to the circle of his own kindred — granting Sophy's claim never perfectly cleared up, but subject to a tormenting doubt — her future equally assured — her possible rights equally established — Darrell's conscience and pride reconciled to each other. And how, even but as wife to his young kinsman, he would learn to love one so exquisitely endearing!" [Lady Montfort paused a moment, and then resumed.] "When I heard that Mr. Darrell was about to marry again, my project was necessarily arrested."

"Certainly," said George, "if he formed new ties, Sophy would be less an object in his existence, whether or not he recognised her birth. The alliance between her and Lionel would lose many of its advantages; and any address to him on Sophy's behalf would become yet more ungraciously received."

LADY MONTFORT. — "In that case I had resolved to adopt Sophy as my own child; lay by from my abundant income an ample dowry for her; and whether Mr. Darrell ever know it or not, at least I should have the secret joy to think that I was saving him from the risk of remorse hereafter — should she be, as we believe, his daughter's child, and have been thrown upon the world destitute; — yes, the secret joy of feeling that I was sheltering, fostering as a mother, one whose rightful home might be with him who in my childhood sheltered, fostered me!"

GEORGE (much affected). — "How, in proportion as we know you, the beauty which you veil from the world outshines that which you cannot prevent the world from seeing! But you must not let this grateful enthusiasm blind your better judgment. You think these young persons are beginning to be really attached to each other.

Then it is the more necessary that no time should be lost in learning how Mr. Darrell would regard such a marriage. I do not feel so assured of his consent as you appear to do. At all events, this should be ascertained before their happiness is seriously involved. I agree with you that Lionel is the best intermediator to plead for Sophy; and his very generosity in urging her prior claim to a fortune that might otherwise pass to him is likely to have weight with a man so generous himself as Guy Darrell is held to be. But does Lionel yet know all? Have you yet ventured to confide to him, or even to Sophy herself, the nature of her claim on the man who so proudly denies it?"

"No—I deemed it due to Sophy's pride of sex to imply to her that she would, in fortune and in social position, be entitled to equality with those whom she might meet here. And that is true, if only as the child whom I adopt and enrich. I have not said more. And only since Lionel has appeared has she ever seemed interested in anything that relates to her parentage. From the recollection of her father she naturally shrinks—she never mentions his name. But two days ago she did ask timidly, and with great change of countenance, if it was through her mother that she was entitled to a rank higher than she had hitherto known; and when I answered 'yes,' she sighed, and said 'But my dear grandfather never spoke to me of her; he never even saw my mother.'"

GEORGE.—"And you, I suspect, do not much like to talk of that mother. I have gathered from you, unawares to yourself, that she was not a person you could highly praise; and to me, as a boy, she seemed, with all her timidity, wayward and deceitful."

LADY MONTFORT.—"Alas! how bitterly she must have suffered—and how young she was! But you are right; I cannot speak to Sophy of her mother, the subject is connected with so much sorrow. But I told her 'that she should know all soon,' and she said, with a sweet and melancholy patience, 'When my poor grandfather will be by to hear; I can wait.'"

GEORGE.—"But is Lionel, with his quick intellect and busy imagination, equally patient? Does he not guess at the truth? You have told him that you do meditate a project which affects Guy Darrell, and required his promise not to divulge to Darrell his visits in this house."

LADY MONTFORT — "He knows that Sophy's paternal grandfather was William
Losely. From your uncle he heard William Losely's story, and — "

GEORGE. — "My uncle Alban?"

LADY MOSTFORT. — "Yes; the Colonel was well acquainted with the elder Losely in former days, and spoke of him to Lionel with great affection. It seems that Lionel's father knew him also, and thoughtlessly involved him in his own pecuniary difficulties. Lionel was not long a visitor here before he asked me abruptly if Mr. Waife's real name was not Losely. I was obliged to own it, begging him not at present to question me further. He said then, with much emotion, that he had an hereditary debt to discharge to William Losely, and that he was the last person who ought to relinquish belief in the old man's innocence of the crime for which the law had condemned him, or to judge him harshly if the innocence were not substantiated. You remember with what eagerness he joined in your search, until you positively forbade his interposition, fearing that should our poor friend hear of inquiries instituted by one whom he could not recognise as a friend, and might possibly consider an emissary of his son's, he would take yet greater pains to conceal himself. But from the moment that Lionel learned that Sophy's grandfather was William Losely, his manner to Sophy became yet more tenderly respectful. He has a glorious nature, that young man! But did your uncle never speak to you of William Losely?"

"No. I am not surprised at that. My uncle Alban avoids 'painful subjects.' I am only surprised that he should have revived a painful subject in talk to Lionel. But I now understand why, when Waife first heard my name, he seemed affected, and why he so specially enjoined me never to mention or describe him to my friends and relations. Then Lionel knows Losely's story, but not his son's connection with Darrell?"

"Certainly not. He knows but what is generally said in the world, that Darrell's daughter eloped with a Mr. Hammond, a man of inferior birth, and died abroad, leaving but one child, who is also dead. Still Lionel does suspect,—my very injunctions of secrecy must make him more than suspect, that the Loselys are somehow or other mixed up With Darrell's family history. Hush! I hear his voice yonder—they approach."

"My dear cousin, let it be settled between us, then, that you frankly and without delay communicate to Lionel the whole truth, so far as it is known to us, and put it to him how best and most touchingly to move Mr. Darrell towards her, of whom we hold him to be the natural protector. I will write to my uncle to return to England that he may assist us in the same good work. Meanwhile, I shall have only good tidings to communicate to Sophy in my new hopes to discover her grandfather through Merle."

Here, as the sun was setting, Lionel and Sophy came in sight,— above their heads, the western clouds bathed in gold and purple. Sophy, perceiving George, bounded forwards, and reached his side, breathless.

CHAPTER V.

LIONEL HAUGHTON HAVING LOST HIS HEART, IT IS NO LONGER A QUESTION OF WHAT HE WILL DO WITH IT. BUT WHAT WILL BE DONE WITH IT IS A VERY GRAVE QUESTION INDEED.

Lionel forestalled Lady Montfort in the delicate and embarrassing subject which her cousin had urged her to open. For while George, leading away Sophy, informed her of his journey to Norwich, and his interview with Merle, Lionel drew. Lady Montfort into the house, and with much agitation, and in abrupt hurried accents, implored her to withdraw the promise which forbade him to inform his benefactor how and where his time had been spent of late. He burst forth with a declaration of that love with which Sophy had inspired him, and which Lady Montfort could not be but prepared to hear. "Nothing," said he, "but a respect for her more than filial anxiety at this moment could have kept my heart thus long silent. But that heart is so deeply pledged—so utterly hers—that it has grown an ingratitude, a disrespect—to my generous kinsman, to conceal from him any longer the feelings which must colour my whole future existence. Nor can I say to her, 'Can you return my affection?— will you listen to my vows?—will you accept them at the altar?'—until I have won, as I am sure to win, the approving consent of my more than father."

"You feel sure to win that consent, in spite of the stain on her grandfather's name?"

"When Darrell learns that, but for my poor father's fault, that name might be spotless now!—yes! I am not Mr. Darrell's son—the transmitter of his line. I believe yet that he will form new ties. By my mother's side I have no ancestors to boast of; and you have owned to me that Sophy's mother was of gentle birth. Alban Morley told me, when I last saw him, that Darrell wishes me to marry, and leaves me free to choose my bride. Yes; I have no doubt of Mr. Darrell's consent. My dear mother will welcome to her heart the prize so coveted by mine; and Charles Haughton's son will have a place at his hearth for the old age of William Losely. Withdraw your interdict at once, dearest Lady Montfort, and confide to me all that you have hitherto left unexplained, but have promised to reveal when the time came. The time has come."

"It has come," said Lady Montfort, solemnly; "and Heaven grant that it may bear the blessed results which were in my thoughts when I took Sophy as my own adopted daughter, and hailed in yourself the reconciler of conflicting circumstance. Not under this roof should you woo William Losely's grandchild. Doubly are you bound to ask Guy Darrell's consent and blessing. At his hearth woo your Sophy — at his hands ask a bride in his daughter's child."

And to her wondering listener, Cayoline Montford told her grounds for the belief that connected the last of the Darrells with the convict's grandchild.

CHAPTER VI.

CREDULOUS CRYSTAL-SEERS, YOUNG LOVERS, AND GRAVE WISE MEN — ALL IN THE SAME CATEGORY.

George Morley set out the next day for Norwich, in which antique city, ever since the 'Dane peopled it, some wizard or witch, star-reader, or crystal-seer' has enjoyed a mysterious renown, perpetuating thus through all change in our land's social progress the long line of Vala and Saga, who came with the Raven and Valkyr from Scandinavian pine shores. Merle's reserve vanished on the perusal of Sophy's letter to him. He informed George that Waife declared he had plenty of money, and had even forced a loan upon Merle; but that he liked an active, wandering life; it kept him from thinking, and that a pedlar's pack would give him a license for vagrancy, and a budget to defray its expenses; that Merle had been consulted by him in the choice of light popular wares, and as to the route he might find the most free from competing rivals. Merle willingly agreed to accompany George in quest of the wanderer, whom, by the help of his crystal, he seemed calmly sure he could track and discover. Accordingly, they both set out in the somewhat devious and desultory road which Merle, who had some old acquaintances amongst the ancient profession of hawkers, had advised Waife to take. But Merle, unhappily confiding more in his crystal than Waife's steady adherence to the chart prescribed, led the Oxford scholar the life of a will-of-the-wisp; zigzag, and shooting to and fro, here and there, till, just when George had lost all patience, Merle chanced to see, not in the crystal, a pelerine on the neck of a farmer's daughter, which he was morally certain he had himself selected for Waife's pannier. And the girl stating in reply to his inquiry that her father had bought that pelerine as a present for her, not many days before, of a pedlar in a neighbouring town, to the market of which the farmer resorted weekly, Merle cast an horary scheme, and finding the Third House (of short journeys) in favourable aspect to the Seventh House (containing the object desired), and in conjunction with the Eleventh House (friends), he gravely informed the scholar that their toils were at an end, and that the Hour and the Man were at hand. Not over-sanguine, George consigned himself and the seer to an early train, and reached the famous town of Oazelford, whither, when the chronological order of our narrative (which we have so far somewhat forestalled) will permit, we shall conduct the inquisitive reader.

Meanwhile Lionel, subscribing without a murmur to Lady Montfort's injunction to see Sophy no more till Darrell had been conferred with and his consent won, returned to his lodgings in London, sanguine of success, and flushed with joy. His intention was to set out at once to Fawley; but on reaching town he found there a few lines from Dairell himself, in reply to a long and affectionate letter which Lionel had written a few days before asking permission to visit the old manor-house; for amidst all his absorbing love for Sophy, the image of his lonely benefactor in that gloomy hermitage often rose before him. In these lines, Darrell, not unkindly, but very peremptorily, declined Lionel's overtures.

"In truth, my dear young kinsman," wrote the recluse — "in truth I am, with slowness, and with frequent relapses, labouring through convalescence from a moral fever. My nerves are yet unstrung. I am as one to whom is prescribed the most complete repose; — the visits, even of friends the dearest, forbidden as a perilous excitement. The sight of you — of any one from the great world — but especially of one whose rich vitality of youth and hope affronts and mocks my own fatigued exhaustion, would but irritate, unsettle, torture me. When I am quite well I will ask you to come. I shall enjoy your visit. Till then, on no account, and on no pretext, let my morbid ear catch the sound of your footfall on my quiet floor. Write to me often, but tell me nothing of the news and gossip of the world. Tell me only of yourself, your studies, your thoughts, your sentiments, your wishes. Nor forget my injunctions. Marry young, marry for love; let no ambition of power, no greed of gold, ever mislead you into giving to your life a companion who is not the half of your soul. Choose with the heart of a man; I know that you will choose with the self-esteem of a gentleman; and be assured beforehand of the sympathy and sanction of your 'CHURLISH BUT LOVING KINSMAN.'"

After this letter, Lionel felt that, at all events, he could not at once proceed to the old manor-house in defiance of its owner's prohibition. He wrote briefly, entreating Darrell to forgive him if he persisted in the prayer to be received at Fawley, stating that his desire for a personal interview was now suddenly become special and urgent; that it not only concerned himself, but affected his benefactor. By return of post Darrell replied with curt frigidity, repeating, with even sternness, his refusal to receive Lionel, but professing himself ready to attend to all that his kinsman might address to him by letter. "If it be as you state," wrote Darrell, with his habitual irony, "a matter that relates to myself, I claim, as a lawyer for my own affairs—the precaution I once enjoined to my clients—a written brief should always precede a personal consultation."

In fact, the proud man suspected that Lionel had been directly or indirectly addressed on behalf of Jasper Losely; and cerainly that was the last subject on which he would have granted an interview to his young kinsman. Lionel, however; was not perhaps sorry to be thus compelled to trust to writing his own and Sophy's cause. Darrell was one of those men whose presence inspires a certain awe—one of those men whom we feel, upon great occasions, less embarrassed to address by letter than in person. Lionel's pen moved rapidly—his whole heart and soul suffused with feeling—; and, rushing over the page, he reminded Darrell of the day when he had told to the rich man the tale of the lovely wandering child, and how, out of his sympathy for that child, Darrell's approving, fostering tenderness to himself had grown. Thus indirectly to her forlorn condition had he owed the rise in his own fortunes. He went through the story of William Losely as he had gathered it from Alban Morley, and touched pathetically on his own father's share in that dark history. If William Losely really was hurried into crime by the tempting necessity for a comparatively trifling sum, but for Charles Haughton would the necessity have arisen? Eloquently then the lover united grandfather and grandchild in one touching picture—their love for each other, their dependence on each other. He enlarged on Sophy's charming, unselfish, simple, noble character; he told how he had again found her; he dwelt on the refining accomplishments she owed to Lady Montfort's care. How came she with Lady Montfort? Why had Lady Montfort cherished, adopted her? Because Lady Montfort told him how much her own childhood had owed to Darrell; because, should Sophy be, as alleged, the offspring of his daughter, the heiress of his line, Caroline Montfort rejoiced to guard her from danger, save her from poverty, and ultimately thus to fit her to be not only acknowledged with delight, but with pride. Why had he been enjoined not to divulge to Darrell that he had again found, and under Lady Montfort's roof, the child whom, while yet unconscious of her claims, Darrell himself had vainly sought to find, and benevolently designed to succour? Because Lady Montfort wished to fulfil her task- complete Sophy's education, interrupted by grief for her missing grandfather, and obtain indeed, when William Losely again returned, some proofs (if such existed) to corroborate the assertion of Sophy's parentage. "And," added Lionel, "Lady Montfort seems to fear that she has given you some cause of displeasure—what I know not, but which might have induced you to disapprove of the acquaintance I had begun with her. Be that as it may, would you could hear the reverence with which she ever alludes to your worth—the gratitude with which she attests her mother's and her own early obligations to your intellect and heart!" Finally, Lionel wove all his threads of recital into the confession of the deep love into which his romantic memories of Sophy's wandering childhood had been ripened by the sight of her graceful, cultured youth. "Grant," he said, "that her father's tale be false—and no doubt you have sufficient reasons to discredit it—still, if you cannot love her as your daughter's child, receive, know her, I implore—let her love and revere you—as my wife! Leave me to protect her from a lawless father—leave me to redeem, by some deeds of loyalty and honour, any stain that her grandsire's sentence may seem to fix upon our union. Oh! if ambitious before, how ambitious I should be now—to efface for her sake, as for mine, her grandsire's shame, my father's errors! But if, on the other hand, she should, on the requisite inquiries, be proved to descend from your ancestry—your father's blood in her pure veins—I know, alas! then that I should have no right to aspire to such nuptials. Who would even think of her descent from a William Losely? Who would not be too proud to remember only her descent from you? All spots would vanish in the splendour of your renown; the highest in the land would court her alliance. And I am but the pensioner of your bounty, and only on my father's side of gentle origin. But still I think you would not reject me—you would place the future to my credit; and I would wait, wait patiently, till I had won such a soldier's name as would entitle me to mate with a daughter of the Darrells."

Sheet upon sheet the young eloquence flowed on—seeking, with an art of which the writer was unconscious, all the arguments and points of view which might be the most captivating to the superb pride or to the exquisite tenderness which seemed to Lionel the ruling elements of Darrell's character.

He had not to wait long for a reply. At the first glance of the address on its cover, his mind misgave him; the hopes that bad hitherto elated his spirit yielded to abrupt forebodings. Darrell's handwriting was habitually in harmony with the intonations of his voice-singularly clear, formed with a peculiar and original elegance, yet with the undulating ease of a natural, candid, impulsive charac- ter. And that decorous care in such mere trifles as the very sealing of a letter, which, neglected by musing poets and abstracted au- thors, is observable in men of high public station, was in Guy Dar- rell significant of the Patrician dignity that imparted a certain state- liness to his most ordinary actions.

But in the letter which lay in Lionel's hand the writer was scarcely recognisable—the direction blurred, the characters dashed off from a pen fierce yet tremulous; the seal a great blotch of wax; the device of the heron, with its soaring motto, indistinct and mangled, as if the stamping instrument had been plucked wrathfully away before the wax had cooled. And when Lionel opened the letter, the hand- writing within was yet more indicative of mental disorder. The very ink looked menacing and angry- blacker as the pen had been for- cibly driven into the page. "Unhappy boy!" began the ominous epistle, "is it through you that the false and detested woman who has withered up the noon-day of my life seeks to dishonour its blighted close? Talk not to me of Lady Montfort's gratitude and reverence! Talk not to me of her amiable, tender, holy aim, to obtru- de upon my childless house the grand-daughter of a convicted fel- on! Show her these lines, and ask her by what knowledge of my nature she can assume that ignominy to my name would be a bles- sing to my hearth? Ask her, indeed, how she can dare to force herself still upon my thoughts—dare to imagine she can lay me under obligations—dare to think she can be something still in my forlorn existence! Lionel Haughton, I command you in the name of all the dead whom we can claim as ancestors in common, to tear from your heart, as you would tear a thought of disgrace, this image which has bewitched your reason. My daughter, thank Heaven, left no pledge of an execrable union. But a girl who has been brought up by a thief—a girl whom a wretch so lost to honour as Jasper Losely sought to make an instrument of fraud to my harassment and disgrace, be her virtues and beauty what they may, I could not, without intolerable anguish, contemplate as the wife of Lionel Haughton. But receive her as your wife!

"Admit her within these walls! Never, never; I scorn to threaten you with loss of favour, loss of fortune. Marry her if you will. You shall have an ample income secure to you. But from that moment our lives are separated—our relation ceases. You will never again see nor address me. But oh, Lionel, can you—can you inflict upon me this crowning sorrow? Can you, for the sake of a girl of whom you have seen but little, or in the Quixotism of atonement for your father's fault, complete the ingratitude I have experienced from those who owed me most? I cannot think it. I rejoice that you wrote—did not urge this suit in person. I should not have been able to control my passion; we might have parted foes. As it is, I restrain myself with difficulty! That woman, that child, associated thus to tear from me the last affection left to my ruined heart. No! You will not be so cruel! Send this, I command you, to Lady Montfort. See again neither her nor the impostor she has been cherishing for my disgrace. This letter will be your excuse to break off with both—with both. GUY DARRELL."

Lionel was stunned. Not for several hours could he recover self-possession enough to analyse his own emotions, or discern the sole course that lay before him. After such a letter from such a benefactor, no option was left to him. Sophy must be resigned; but the sacrifice crushed him to the earth—crushed the very manhood out of him. He threw himself on the floor, sobbing—sobbing as if body and soul were torn, each from each, in convulsive spasms.

But send this letter to Lady Montfort? A letter so wholly at variance with Darrell's dignity of character—a letter in which rage seemed lashed to unreasoning frenzy. Such bitter language of hate and scorn, and even insult to a woman, and to the very woman who had seemed to Lionel so reverently to cherish the writer's name—so tenderly to scheme for the writer's happiness! Could he obey a command that seemed to lower Darrell even more than it could humble her to whom it was sent?

Yet disobey! What but the letter itself could explain? Ah—and was there not some strange misunderstanding with respect to Lady Montfort, which the letter itself, and nothing but the letter, would enable her to dispel; and if dispelled, might not Darrell's whole mind undergo a change? A flash of joy suddenly broke on his agitated, tempestuous thoughts. He forced himself again to read those blotted impetuous lines. Evidently—evidently, while writing to Lionel—the subject Sophy—the man's wrathful heart had been addressing itself to neither. A suspicion seized him; with that suspicion, hope. He would send the letter, and with but few words from himself—words that revealed his immense despair at the thought of relinquishing Sophy—intimated his belief that Darrell here was, from some error of judgment which Lionel could not comprehend, avenging himself on Lady Montfort; and closed with his prayer to her, if so, to forgive lines coloured by hasty passion, and, for the sake of all, not to disdain that self-vindication which might perhaps yet soften a nature possessed of such depths of sweetness as that which appeared now so cruel and so bitter. He would not yet despond—not yet commission her to give his last farewell to Sophy.

CHAPTER VII.

THE MAN-EATER CONTINUES TO TAKE HIS QUIET STEAK OUT OF DOLLY POOLE; AND IS IN TURN SUBJECTED TO THE ANATOMICAL KNIFE OF THE DISSECTING AUTHOR. TWO TRAPS ARE LAID FOR HIM — ONE BY HIS FELLOW MAN-EATERS — ONE BY THAT DEADLY PERSECUTRIX, THE WOMAN WHO TRIES TO SAVE HIM IN SPITE OF ALL HE CAN DO TO BE HANGED.

Meanwhile the unhappy Adolphus Poole had been the reluctant but unfailing source from which Jasper Losely had weekly drawn the supplies to his worthless and workless existence. Never was a man more constrainedly benevolent, and less recompensed for pecuniary sacrifice by applauding conscience, than the doomed inhabitant of Alhambra Villa. In the utter failure of his attempts to discover Sophy, or to induce Jasper to accept Colonel Morley's proposals, he saw this parasitical monster fixed upon his entrails, like the vulture on those of the classic sufferer in mythological tales. Jasper, indeed, had accommodated himself to this regular and unlaborious mode of gaining "/sa pauvre vie/." To call once a week upon his old acquaintance, frighten him with a few threats, or force a deathlike smile from agonising lips by a few villanous jokes, carry off his four sovereigns, and enjoy himself thereon till pay-day duly returned, was a condition of things that Jasper did not greatly care to improve; and truly had he said to Poole that his earlier energy had left him. As a sensualist of Jasper's stamp grows older and falls lower, indolence gradually usurps the place once occupied by vanity or ambition. Jasper was bitterly aware that his old comeliness was gone; that never more could he ensnare a maiden's heart or a widow's gold. And when this truth was fully brought home to him, it made a strange revolution in all his habits. He cared no longer for dress and gewgaws — sought rather to hide himself than to parade. In the neglect of the person he had once so idolised — in the coarse roughness which now characterised his exterior — there was that sullen despair which the vain only know when what had made

them dainty and jocund is gone for ever. The human mind, in dete-
riorating, fits itself to the sphere into which it declines. Jasper would
not now, if he could, have driven a cabriolet down St. James's Street.
He had taken more and more to the vice of drinking as the excitement of gambling was withdrawn from him. For how gamble with
those who had nothing to lose, and to whom he himself would have
been pigeon, not hawk? And as he found that, on what he thus
drew regularly from Dolly Poole, he could command all the com-
forts that his embruted tastes now desired, so an odd kind of prudence for the first time in his life came with what he chose to consider "a settled income." He mixed with ruffians in their nightly or-
gies; treated them to cheap potations; swaggered, bullied, boasted,
but shared in no project of theirs which might bring into jeopardy
the life which Dolly Poole rendered so comfortable and secure. His
energies, once so restless, were lulled, partly by habitual intoxicati-
on, partly by the physical pains which had nestled themselves into
his robust fibres, efforts of an immense and still tenacious vitality to
throw off diseases repugnant to its native magnificence of health.
The finest constitutions are those which, when once seriously im-
paired, occasion the direst pain; but they also enable the sufferer to
bear pain that would soon wear away the delicate. And Jasper bore
his pains stoutly, though at times they so exasperated his temper,
that woe then to any of his comrades whose want of caution or
respect gave him the occasion to seek relief in wrath! His hand was
as heavy, his arm as stalwart as ever. George Morley had been
rightly informed. Even by burglars and cut-throats, whose dangers
he shunned, while fearlessly he joined their circle, Jasper Losely was
regarded with terror. To be the awe of reckless men, as he had been
the admiration of foolish women, this was delight to his vanity, the
last delight that was left to it. But he thus provoked a danger to
which his arrogance was blind. His boon companions began to
grow tired of him. He had been welcomed to their resort on the
strength of the catchword or passport which confederates at Paris
had communicated to him, and of the reputation for great daring
and small scruple which he took from Cutts, who was of high caste
amongst their mysterious tribes, and who every now and then flitted over the Continent, safe and accursed as the Wandering Jew.
But when they found that this Achilles of the Greeks would only
talk big, and employ his wits on his private exchequer and his

thews against themselves, they began not only to tire of his imperious manner, but to doubt his fidelity to the cause. And, all of a sudden, Cutts, who had at first extolled Jasper as one likely to be a valuable acquisition to the Family of Night, altered his tone, and insinuated that the bravo was not to be trusted; that his reckless temper and incautious talk when drunk would unfit him for a safe accomplice in any skilful project of plunder; and that he was so unscrupulous, and had so little sympathy with their class, that he might be quite capable of playing spy or turning king's evidence; that, in short, it would be well to rid themselves of his domineering presence. Still there was that physical power in this lazy Hercules — still, if the Do-nought, he was so fiercely the Dread- nought — that they did not dare, despite the advantage of numbers, openly to brave and defy him. No one would bell the cat — and such a cat! They began to lay plots to get rid of him through the law. Nothing could be easier to such knowing adepts in guilt than to transfer to his charge any deed of violence one of their own gang had committed — heap damning circumstances round him — privily apprise justice — falsely swear away his life. In short, the man was in their way as a wasp that has blundered into an ants' nest; and, while frightened at the size of the intruder, these honest ants were resolved to get him out of their citadel alive or dead. Probable it was that Jasper Losely would meet with his deserts at last for an offence of which he was as innocent as a babe unborn.

It is at this juncture that we are re-admitted to the presence of Arabella Crane.

She was standing by a window on the upper floor of a house situated in a narrow street. The blind was let down, but she had drawn it a little aside, and was looking out. By the fireside was seated a thin, vague, gnome-like figure, perched comfortless on the edge of a rush-bottomed chair, with its shadowy knees drawn up till they nearly touched its shadowy chin. There was something about the outline of this figure so indefinite and unsubstantial, that you might have taken it for an optical illusion, a spectral apparition on the point of vanishing. This thing was, however, possessed of voice, and was speaking in a low but distinct hissing whisper. As the whisper ended, Arabella Crane, without turning her face, spoke, also under her breath.

"You are sure that, so long as Losely draws this weekly stipend from the man whom he has in his power, he will persist in the same course of life. Can you not warn him of the danger?"

"Peach against pals! I dare not. No trusting him."

"He would come down, mad with brandy, make an infernal row, seize two or three by the throat, dash their heads against each other, blab, bully, and a knife would be out, and a weasand or two cut, and a carcase or so dropped into the Thames—mine certainly—his perhaps."

"You say you can keep back this plot against him for two or three days?"

"For two days—yes. I should be glad to save General Jas. He has the bones of a fine fellow, and if he had not destroyed himself by brandy, he might have been at the top of the tree-in the profession. But he is fit for nothing now."

"Ah! and you say the brandy is killing him?"

"No, he will not be killed by brandy, if he continues to drink it among the same jolly set."

"And if he were left without the money to spend amongst these terrible companions, he would no longer resort to their meetings? You are right there. The same vanity that makes him pleased to be the great man in that society would make him shrink from coming amongst them as a beggar."

"And if he had not the wherewithal to pay the weekly subscription, there would be an excuse to shut the door in his face. All these fellows wish to do is to get rid of him; and if by fair means, there would be no necessity to resort to foul. The only danger would be that from which you have so often saved him. In despair, would he not commit some violent rash action—a street robbery, or something of the kind? He has courage for any violence, but no longer the cool head to plan a scheme which would not be detected. You see I can prevent my pals joining in such risks as he may propose, or letting him (if he were to ask it) into an adventure of their own, for they know that I am a safe adviser; they respect me; the law has never been able to lay hold of me; and when I say to them, 'That fellow drinks, blabs, and boasts, and would bring us all into trouble,' they will have nothing to do with him; but I cannot prevent his doing what he pleases out of his own muddled head, and with his own reckless hand."

"But you will keep in his confidence, and let me know till that he proposes!"

"Yes."

"And meanwhile, he must come to me. And this time I have more hope than ever, since his health gives way, and he is weary of crime itself. Mr. Cutts, come near—softly. Look-nay, nay, he cannot see you from below, and you are screened by the blind. Look, I say, where he sits."

She pointed to a room on the ground-floor in the opposite house, where might be dimly seen a dull red fire in a sordid grate, and a man's form, the head pillowed upon arms that rested on a small table. On the table a glass, a bottle.

"It is thus that his mornings pass," said Arabella Crane, with a wild bitter pity in the tone of her voice. "Look, I say, is he formidable now? can you fear him?"

"Very much indeed," muttered Cutts. "He is only stupefied, and he can shake off a doze as quickly as a bulldog does when a rat is let into his kennel."

"Mr. Cutts, you tell me that he constantly carries about him the same old pocket-book which he says contains his fortune; in other words, the papers that frighten his victim into giving him the money which is now the cause of his danger. There is surely no pocket you cannot pick or get picked, Mr. Cutts? Fifty pounds for that book in three hours."

"Fifty pounds are not enough; the man he sponges on would give more to have those papers in his power."

"Possibly; but Losely has not been dolt enough to trust you sufficiently to enable you to know how to commence negotiations. Even if the man's name and address be amongst those papers, you could

not make use of the knowledge without bringing Jasper himself
upon you; and even if Jasper were out of the way, you would not
have the same hold over his victim; you know not the circumstances; you could make no story out of some incoherent rambling
letters; and the man, who, I can tell you, is by nature a bully, and
strong, compared with any other man but Jasper, would seize you
by the collar; and you would be lucky if you got out of his house
with no other loss than the letters, and no other gain but a broken
bone. Pooh! YOU know all that, or you would have stolen the book,
and made use of it before. Fifty pounds for that book in three hours;
and if Jasper Losely be safe and alive six months hence, fifty pounds
more, Mr. Cutts. See! he stirs not must be fast asleep. Now is the
moment."

"What, in his own room!" said Cutts with contempt. "Why, he
would know who did it; and where should I be to-morrow? No—in
the streets; any one has a right to pick a pocket in the Queen's
highways. In three hours you shall have the book."

CHAPTER VIII.

MERCURY IS THE PATRON DEITY OF MERCANTILE SPECULATORS, AS WELL AS OF CRACK-BRAINED POETS; INDEED, HE IS MUCH MORE FAVOURABLE, MORE A FRIEND AT A PINCH, TO THE FORMER CLASS OF HIS PROTEGES THAN HE IS TO THE LATTER.

"Poolum per hostes mercurius celer,
Denso paventem sustulit aere."

Poole was sitting with his wife after dinner. He had made a good speculation that day; little Johnny would be all the better for it a few years hence, and some other man's little Johnnys all the worse—but each for himself in this world! Poole was therefore basking in the light of his gentle helpmate's approving smile. He had taken all extra glass of a venerable port-wine, which had passed to his cellar from the bins of Uncle Sam. Commercial prosperity without, conjugal felicity within, the walls of Alhambra Villa; surely Adolphus Poole is an enviable man! Does he look so? The ghost of what he was but a few months ago! His cheeks have fallen in; his clothes hang on him like bags; there is a worried, haggard look in his eyes, a nervous twitch in his lips, and every now and then he looks at the handsome Parisian clock on the chimneypiece, and then shifts his posture, snubs his connubial angel, who asks "what ails him?" refills his glass, and stares on the fire, seeing strange shapes in the mobile aspects of the coals.

To-morrow brings back this weekly spectre! To-morrow Jasper Losely, punctual to the stroke of eleven, returns to remind him of that past which, if revealed, will blast the future. And revealed it might be any hour despite the bribe for silence which he must pay with his own hands, under his own roof. Would he trust another with the secret of that payment?—horror! Would he visit Losely at his own lodging, and pay him there?—murder! Would he appoint him somewhere in the streets—run the chance of being seen with such a friend? Respectability confabulating with offal?—disgrace! And Jasper had on the last two or three visits been peculiarly disagreeable. He had talked loud. Poole feared that his wife might have her ear at the keyhole. Jasper had seen the parlour-maid in the passage as he went out, and caught her round the waist. The parlourmaid had complained to Mrs. Poole, and said she would leave if so insulted by such an ugly blackguard. Alas! what the poor lady-killer has come to! Mrs. Poole had grown more and more inquisitive and troublesome on the subject of such extraordinary visits; and now, as her husband stirred the fire-having roused her secret ire by his previous unmanly snubbings, and Mrs. Poole being one of those incomparable wives who have a perfect command of temper, who never reply to angry words at the moment, and who always, with exquisite calm and self-possession, pay off every angry word by an amiable sting at a right moment—Mrs. Poole, I say, thus softly said:

"Sammy, duck, we know what makes oo so cross; but it shan't vex oo long, Sammy. That dreadful man comes to-morrow. He always comes the same day of the week."

"Hold your tongue, Mrs. Poole."

"Yes, Sammy, dear, I'll hold my tongue. But Sammy shan't be imposed upon by mendicants; for I know he is a mendicant—one of those sharpers or blacklegs who took oo in, poor innocent Sam, in oo wild bachelor days, and oo good heart can't bear to see him in distress; but there must be an end to all things."

"Mrs. Poole—Mrs. Poole-will you stop your fool's jaw or not?"

"My poor dear hubby," said the angel, squeezing out a mild tear, "oo will be in good hands to advise oo; for I've been and told Pa!"

"You have," faltered Poole, "told your father—you have!" and the expression of his face became so ghastly that Mrs. Poole grew seriously terrified. She had long felt that there was something very suspicious in her husband's submission to the insolence of so rude a visitor. But she knew that he was not brave; the man might intimidate him by threats of personal violence. The man might probably be some poor relation, or some one whom Poole had ruined, either in bygone discreditable sporting 'days, or in recent respectable mercantile speculations. But at that ghastly look a glimpse of the real truth broke upon her; and she stood speechless and appalled. At this moment there was a loud ring at the street-door bell. Poole gathered himself up, and staggered out of the room into the passage.

His wife remained without motion; for the first time she conceived a fear of her husband. Presently she heard a harsh female voice in the hall, and then a joyous exclamation from Poole himself. Recovered by these unexpected sounds, she went mechanically forth into the passage, just in time to see the hems of a dark-grey dress disappearing within Poole's study, while Poole, who had opened the study-door, and was bowing-in the iron-grey dress obsequiously, turned his eye towards his wife, and striding towards her for a moment, whispered, "Go up-stairs and stir not," in a tone so unlike his usual gruff accents of command, that it cowed her out of the profound contempt with which she habitually received, while smilingly obeying, his marital authority.

Poole, vanishing into his study, carefully closed his door, and would have caught his lady visitor by both her hands; but she waived him back, and, declining a seat, remained sternly erect.

"Mr. Poole, I have but a few words to say. The letters which gave Jasper Losely the power to extort money from you are no longer in his possession; they are in mine. You need fear him no more—you will fee him no more."

"Oh!" cried Poole, falling on his knees, "the blessing of a father of a family—a babe not six weeks born—be on your blessed, blessed head!"

"Get up, and don't talk nonsense. I do not give you these papers at present, nor burn them. Instead of being in the power of a muddled, irresolute drunkard, you are in the power of a vigilant, clear-brained woman. You are in my power, and you will act as I tell you."

"You can ask nothing wrong, I am sure," said Poole, his grateful enthusiasm much abated. "Command me; but the papers can be of no use to you; I will pay for them handsomely."

"Be silent and listen. I retain these papers-first, because Jasper Losely must not know that they ever passed to my hands; secondly, because you must inflict no injury on Losely himself. Betray me to him, or try to render himself up to the law, and the documents will be used against you ruthlessly. Obey, and you have nothing to fear, and nothing to pay. When Jasper Losely calls on you tomorrow, ask him to show you the letters. He cannot; he will make excuses. Decline peremptorily, but not insultingly (his temper is fierce), to pay him farther. He will perhaps charge you with having hired some one to purloin his pocket-book; let him think it. Stop—your window here opens on the ground—a garden without: —Ah! have three of the police in that garden, in sight of the window. Point to them if he threaten you; summon them to your aid, or pass out to them, if he actually attempt violence. But when he has left the house, you must urge no charge against him; he must be let off unscathed. You can be at no loss for excuse in this mercy; a friend of former times— needy, unfortunate, whom habits of drink maddened for the moment— necessary to eject him—inhuman to prosecute—any story you please. The next day you can, if you choose, leave London for a short time; I advise it. But his teeth will be drawn; he will most probably never trouble you again. I know his character. There, I have done; open the door, sir."

CHAPTER IX.

THE WRECK AND THE LIFE-BOAT IN A FOG.

The next day, a little after noon, Jasper Losely, coming back from Alhambra Villa—furious, desperate, knowing not where to turn for bread, or on whom to pour his rage—beheld suddenly, in a quiet, half-built street, which led from the suburb to the New Road, Arabella Crane standing right in his path. She had emerged from one of the many straight intersecting roads which characterise that crude nebula of a future city; and the woman and the man met thus face to face; not another passer-by visible in the thoroughfare;—at a distance the dozing hack cab-stand; round and about them carcases of brick and mortar—some with gaunt scaffolding fixed into their ribs, and all looking yet more weird in their raw struggle into shape through the living haze of a yellow fog.

Losely, seeing Arabella thus planted in his way, recoiled; and the superstition in which he had long associated her image with baffled schemes and perilous hours sent the wrathful blood back through his veins so quickly that be heard his heart beat!

MRS. CRANE.—"SO! You see we cannot help meeting, Jasper dear, do what you will to shun me."

LOSELY." I—I—you always startle me so!—you are in town, then?—to stay?—your old quarters?"

MRS. CRANE.—"Why ask? You cannot wish to know where I am—you would not call. But how fares it?—what do you do?—how do you live? You look ill—Poor Jasper."

LOSELY (fiercely).—"Hang your pity, and give me some money."

MRS. CRANE (calmly laying her lean hand on the arm which was darted forward more in menace than entreaty, and actually terrifying the Gladiator as she linked that deadly arm into her own).—"I said you would always find me when at the worst of your troubles. And so, Jasper, it shall be till this right hand of yours is powerless as the clay at our feet. Walk—walk; you are not afraid of me?—walk on, tell me all. Where have you just been?"

Jasper, therewith reminded of his wrongs, poured out a volley of abuse on Poole, communicating to Mrs. Crane the whole story of his claims on that gentleman—the loss of the pocket-book filched from him, and Poole's knowledge that he was thus disarmed.

"And the coward," said he, grinding his teeth, "got out of his window —and three policemen in his garden. He must have bribed a pickpocket— low knave that he is. But I shall find out—and then—"

"And then, Jasper, how will you be better off?—the letters are gone; and Poole has you in his power if you threaten him again. Now, hark you; you did not murder the Italian who was found stabbed in the fields yonder a week ago; L100 reward for the murderer?"

"I—no. How coldly you ask! I have hit hard in fair fight; murdered— never. If ever I take to that, I shall begin with Poole."

"But I tell you, Jasper, that you are suspected of that murder; that you will be accused of that murder; and if I had not thus fortunately met you, for that murder you would be tried and hanged."

"Are you serious? Who could accuse me?"

"Those who know that you are not guilty—those who could make you appear so—the villains with whom you horde, and drink and brawl! Have I ever been wrong in my warnings yet?"

"This is too horrible," faltered Losely, thinking not of the conspiracy against his life, but of her prescience in detecting it. "It must be witchcraft, and nothing else. How could you learn what you tell me?"

"That is my affair; enough for you that I am right. Go no more to those black haunts; they are even now full of snares and pitfalls for you. Leave London, and you are safe. Trust to me."

"And where shall I go?"

"Look you, Jasper; you have worn out this old world no refuge for you but the new. Whither went your father, thither go you. Consent, and you shall not want. You cannot discover Sophy. You have failed in all attempts on Darrell's purse. But agree to sail to Australasia, and I will engage to you an income larger than you say you extorted from Poole, to be spent in those safer shores."

"And you will go with me, I suppose," said Losely, with ungracious sullenness.

"Go with you, as you please. Be where you are—yes." The ruffian bounded with rage and loathing.

"Woman, cross me no more, or I shall be goaded into—"

"Into killing me—you dare not! Meet my eye if you can—you dare not! Harm me, yea a hair of my head, and your moments are numbered!—your doom sealed. Be we two together in a desert—not a human eye to see the deed —not a human ear to receive my groan, and still I should stand by your side unharmed. I, who have returned the wrongs received from you, by vigilant, untiring benefits—I, who have saved you from so many enemies, and so many dangers—I, who, now when all the rest of earth shun you— when all other resource fails-I, who now say to you, 'Share my income, but be honest!' I receive injury from that hand. No; the guilt would be too unnatural—Heaven would not permit it. Try, and your arm will fall palsied by your side!"

Jasper's bloodshot eyes dropped beneath the woman's fixed and scorching gaze, and his lips, white and tremulous, refused to breathe the fierce curse into which his brutal nature concentrated its fears and its hate. He walked on in gloomy silence; but some words she had let fall suggested a last resort to his own daring.

She had urged him to quit the old world for the new, but that had been the very proposition conveyed to him from Darrell. If that proposition, so repugnant to the indolence that had grown over him, must be embraced, better at least sail forth alone, his own master, than be the dependent slave of this abhorred and persecuting benefactress. His despair gave him the determination he had hitherto lacked. He would seek Darrell himself, and make the best compromise he could. This resolve passed into his mind as he stalked on through the yellow fog, and his nerves recovered from their irritation, and his thoughts regained something of their ancient craft as the idea of escaping from Mrs. Crane's vigilance and charity assumed a definite shape.

"Well," said he at length, dissimulating his repugnance, and with an effort at his old half-coaxing, half-rollicking tones, "you certainly are the best of creatures; and, as you say,

'Had I a heart for falsehood framed, I ne'er could injure you,'

ungrateful dog though I may seem, and very likely am. I own I have a horror of Australasia—such a long sea-voyage! New scenes no longer attract me; I am no longer young, though I ought to be; but if you insist on it, and will really condescend to accompany me in spite of all my sins to you, why, I can make up my mind. And as to honesty, ask those infernal rascals, who, you say, would swear away my life, and they will tell you that I have been as innocent as a lamb since my return to England; and that is my guilt in their villanous eyes. As long as that infamous Poole gave me enough for my humble wants, I was a reformed man. I wish to keep reformed. Very little suffices for me now. As you say, Australasia may be the best place for me. When shall we go?"

"Are you serious?"

"To be sure."

"Then I will inquire the days on which the vessels sail. You can call on me at my own old home, and all shall be arranged. Oh, Jasper Losely, do not avoid this last chance of escape from the perils that gather round you."

"No; I am sick of life—of all things except repose. Arabella, I suffer horrible pain."

He groaned, for he spoke truly. At that moment the gnaw of the monster anguish, which fastens on the nerves like a wolf's tooth, was so keen that he longed to swell his groan into a roar. The old fable of Hercules in the poisoned tunic was surely invented by some skilled physiologist, to denote the truth that it is only in the strongest frames that pain can be pushed into its extremest torture. The heart of the grim woman was instantly and thoroughly softened. She paused; she made him lean on her arm; she wiped the drops from his brow; she addressed him in the most soothing tones of pity. The spasm passed away suddenly as it does in neuralgic agonies, and with it any gratitude or any remorse in the breast of the sufferer.

"Yes," he said, "I will call on you; but meanwhile I am without a farthing. Oh, do not fear that if you helped me now, I should again shun you. I have no other resource left; nor have I now the spirit I once had. I no longer now laugh at fatigue and danger."

"But will you swear by all that you yet hold sacred—if, alas! there be aught which is sacred to you—that you will not again seek the company of those men who are conspiring to entrap you into the hangman's hands?"

"Seek them again, the ungrateful cowardly blackguards! No, no; I promise you that—solemnly; it is medical aid that I want; it is rest, I tell you—rest, rest, rest." Arabella Crane drew forth her purse. "Take what you will," said she gently. Jasper, whether from the desire to deceive her, or because her alms were so really distasteful to his strange kind of pride that he stinted to bare necessity the appeal to them, contented himself with the third or fourth of the sovereigns that the purse contained, and after a few words of thanks and promises, he left her side, and soon vanished in the fog that grew darker and darker as the night-like wintry day deepened over the silenced thoroughfares.

The woman went her way through the mists, hopeful—through the mists went the man, hopeful also. Recruiting himself by slight food and strong drink at a tavern on his road, he stalked on to Darrell's house in Carlton Gardens; and, learning there that Darrell was at Fawley, hastened to the station from which started the train to the town nearest to the old Manor-house; reached that town safely, and there rested for the night.